FLYING TO HEAVEN

In 1785, Susan Woodford and her invalid mother become penniless and travel to Bath for sanctuary. The flippant balloonist they meet en route is Tom, the Earl of Dearham. They lodge with his Aunt Mary, and Susan is dismayed to learn that they are his dependants. But when she goes up in his balloon and it is swept away to Wales, they fall in love on the dangerous trek home with drovers.

Books by Anne Holman
in the Linford Romance Library:

SAIL AWAY TO LOVE
HER HEART'S DESIRE

ANNE HOLMAN

FLYING TO HEAVEN

Complete and Unabridged

LINFORD
Leicester

First published in Great Britain in 1998
under the title of
'The Wings Of Love'

First Linford Edition
published 1999

British Library CIP Data

Holman, Anne
Flying to heaven.—Large print ed.—
Linford romance library
1. Love stories
2. Large type books
I. Title
823.9′14 [F]

ISBN 0–7089–5547–9

Published by
F. A. Thorpe (Publishing) Ltd.
Anstey, Leicestershire

Set by Words & Graphics Ltd.
Anstey, Leicestershire
Printed and bound in Great Britain by
T. J. International Ltd., Padstow, Cornwall

This book is printed on acid-free paper

1

'Oh, dear me, I feel as though this tiresome journey will never end,' Lady Lavinia said and gave a weary sigh. Her face, like a shrivelled peach peered out from under her bonnet. 'How much farther is it, Susan?'

'I cannot say exactly, Mama. I think we must be getting near Bath.'

Susan Woodford leaned forward to adjust the rug covering her mother's knees, and wondered why Mama was not feeling the heat. The air was stifling in the creaky coach. The October sun was strong enough to burn her skin, but she dare not open a window. If Mama suffered a draught it might lead to a chill, and they simply could not afford for her to become ill again.

Susan looked out of the window at the wispy clouds over the Downs which appeared like giant white brush strokes over a brilliant blue sky. Penned in, she watched with envy a flock of migratory swallows swooping and gliding freely. She was in a sense migrating, too, travelling far from the bustling crowds and odours of London streets, away from the raucous cries of the muffin, shrimp and watercress sellers, and away from an evil creditor.

With an involuntary shudder she prayed they had successfully escaped at last from August Borman's clutches. As a gambling debt, he had taken all Papa's money and their house, leaving them practically naught to live on. Ruined, her father had shot himself.

Mama had fallen ill from the constant worry and hardship of being married to a gambling man, and was now left a poor widow, which meant her nineteen-year-old daughter, Susan, had to cope with their ruin as best she could. Having harmed her family, August Borman's lecherous eyes then turned towards Susan. Fear made her decide that before he laid his hands on her, they must escape.

Although well brought up, Susan was not over-protected. Many a time she'd gone to the market with their maid and seen the wretched poor in the streets. However few pence she'd had, she'd always made sure one penny went into the hand of a beggar. But now their money had almost gone. Scraping together their last sovereigns Susan had hired this old coach to take them to the refuge her mama's late sister's husband, the Earl of Dearham, was providing.

Although the earl hadn't replied to her begging letters personally, his steward had written back and sent her an address in Bath where they could lodge. For the hundredth time since they'd left London, she wondered, had she done the right thing casting herself and her mama into the unknown? Curls falling from under her wide-brimmed hat slid around her slender neck as she gave a sigh.

At least they had somewhere to go. Sitting erect, and giving a quick brush to remove any travel dust from her white puffed-out scarf, she smiled encouragingly at Mama.

Clean and fresh, the countryside sparkled after the shower. The sunlight made the yellow, russet and blazing red trees appear on fire. For someone born and brought up in the great City of London, the country seemed like being in Paradise. But Susan couldn't help also feeling as insecure as one of the falling leaves being blown hither and thither in the lively wind.

She started when the other person in the carriage, Mama's young servant, Betty, gave a loud yawn. Lisping through some missing teeth Betty remarked, 'Gawd, I hopes we are not going to fall to bits afore we gets there, with all this bumpin' about!'

Susan's strained expression relaxed into a warm smile for the simple-minded girl. Years ago, Betty had been given a good home by Lady Lavinia, who'd taken her from the orphanage when she was small and frightened.

Betty had thrived to become a strapping girl, and was devoted to her mistress. She liked Susan, too, and was happy when the young mistress suggested she went with them to Bath.

The passengers suddenly felt the carriage's rocking motion increase. The horses had become frisky. The swish of the whip sounded as the driver barked a command. The carriage gave a sharp jolt, and Susan grasped the squabs to steady herself as Betty lurched forward.

'Lordy! What the . . . ooo-er!' Betty exclaimed.

Lady Lavinia looked aghast at her maid.

'Betty what are you doing sitting on the carriage floor?'

'It's them 'orses dancin' about, ma'am.'

'Betty, really!'

Lady Lavinia had still not quite accustomed herself to the coarse orphanage language her maid produced at times. But she pressed her lips together knowing Betty did her best, and she could not afford a proper lady's maid.

Hiding her amusement, Susan slid along the seat to steady her mother's frail body in case she, too, landed on the carriage boards.

'What in heaven's name is happening? What is exciting the horses?' Mama demanded to know.

Were they about to be overturned by the road's potholes? Susan gave a shiver, wishing the driver had not selected the Sandy Lane route, which he said would have few carriages on it, but there was always the danger they might be accosted by footpads. With her arm around her mother, Susan turned her head to peer out of the carriage window. She could see nothing on the road. Then her eyes glanced upwards.

'Oh, good gracious!'

Susan's head spun. She blinked, twice. Above them in the sky and appearing to be flying straight at them was an enormous, brightly-coloured balloon! Her eyes opened wide, her palms pricked with fear as it seemed as though the contraption might land on them! No wonder the horses were in a frenzy.

While Susan continued to support her mother, she stared with amazement at it. She'd heard of flying balloons, of course. They were all the rage. But actually seeing it almost on top of them was fantastic. As she watched it sail overhead, she saw a man riding in a basket held by the netting underneath. He was busy tipping out all manner of items: bags, assorted boxes, bottles, even a large barometer. How irresponsible, how wasteful he was!

Spellbound, she propped her mother up in the corner of the carriage, and slid to open the window then stuck her head out to watch him fling off his hat, then his greatcoat and boots to throw them all overboard. Her eyes widened farther. She was flabbergasted to observe, before she had time to consider what she was watching, that he had cast off his breeches, too!

Susan's cheeks reddened as she stared up at the handsome man. He had the gall to look down at her uplifted eyes and give her a wide grin before he disappeared out of sight. The next moment, the coachman lost his battle with the horses who sprang forward, taking the coach like a giant ball after them. By the time the cursing driver had managed to gain control of his team again and the snorting animals came to a quivering stop, the ladies inside the coach were badly shaken.

Susan was the first to find her voice.

'Do stop your shrieking, Betty. Find the smelling salts! Can't you see Mama has fainted!'

Seeing Betty administering to her mistress, Susan's next concern was to find that flying man who'd so nearly caused a fatal accident. While the coachman was calming the horses she would tell him what she thought of his reckless behaviour.

Although feeling wobbly at the knees, she tripped down the coach steps.

Possessing only a small neat figure, she was nevertheless used to confronting bailiffs, and market traders who overpriced their inferior wares, so the prospect of reprimanding a mere balloonist did not deter her. How dare he frighten passengers on the King's highway!

Grasping her billowing skirts in one hand, and her hat with the other, she started marching along the road to where she could see the great envelope had become stuck over a copse of tall trees. Overhead, flapping birds circled in distress around their disturbed rookery. In the distance she heard dogs barking and other animal noises coming from a nearby farm. The inconsiderate man's balloon had caused pandemonium.

As Susan opened a gate and began to walk purposefully across a meadow to accost the wrecker she watched the balloon quivering violently in its death throes, and with a final piercing hiss of gas it began to shrivel. She hadn't noticed the mud patches until she trod in one.

She slowed her step wondering if she should abandon her quest before her one and only decent winter gown became soiled, too. But although she'd not spotted him, she instinctively knew the flyer had seen her, and she would look foolish if she turned back. So treading more carefully she proceeded.

Coming up close to the trees she felt his presence, but still hadn't seen him. Tom, however, could see the sun highlighting her graceful figure as he hid in the branches. As she seemed intent on finding him, he called, 'Are you looking for me, ma'am?'

His assured, cultured voice took Susan by surprise and, stepping backwards, she put her hand over her eyes trying to locate him high up in the oak. Ah, there he was! Devilishly intelligent eyes sparkled from his good-looking face, but he looked far from contrite about the havoc he'd caused, and she was not going to conduct his dressing down while he was up in the air. Susan swallowed then took in air to shout.

'You know perfectly well I've come to speak to you, sir.'

'Awkward, ma'am,' he replied with an infuriating grin.

'Come down at once! I'm in a hurry to resume my journey.'

She did not hear his reply because she became aware of thundering hooves behind her. Turning, she found herself facing a herd of cattle advancing at the trot. Dismay hit her. She'd no knowledge of how to deal with farm animals, and climbing trees was not one of her accomplishments.

'Help!' she shrieked. 'Bulls are after me!'

But when the great beasts came within a few feet of her they stopped. Twenty pairs of eyes stared while the animals' heads bobbed as they dribbled at the intruder in their field. Her alarm turned to panic as a great white figure swung down from the tree and dropped lightly by her side. He was a great deal taller than she'd imagined he would be. His fine physique was quite apparent in his undergarments! He gave her a saucy wink.

'Those bulls, ma'am, are cows, and are not dangerous.'

Picking up a stout branch, he snapped it deftly over his thigh and holding a shorter piece he began to wave it at the animals.

'Buttercup, take your troop off!'

He gave the animal with a bell around its neck a hearty slap on its rump, which sent her ambling away, with the rest of the herd following. He then gave Susan a devastating smile which took her breath away.

'Now you know, ma'am,' he said as she stood goggling at him in his underclothes, 'why I was reluctant to show myself.'

Struggling to compose herself she tried to remember why she was there. Making herself stand as tall as she could beside his towering figure, she scolded, 'Sir, do you realise that you almost caused a fatal accident with your, er, conveyance,' she pointed to the remains of his balloon.

His fingers swept back a thick flop of hair from his forehead, which immediately fell back again. He smiled again.

'Ma'am, I assure you my aerostatic machine is as harmless as that herd of cows,' he said.

His flippancy annoyed her.

'Harmless you say?' She'd raised the pitch of her voice. 'If our terrified horses had overturned our carriage you could have harmed Mama!'

She glared at him.

'As if she hasn't suffered enough recently.'

The smile left his face. He was just as handsome minus it.

'She has? Indeed I wouldn't wish to add to her, um . . . ?'

'Loss.'

'Ah, yes. I'm greatly sorry to hear of her loss.'

His deep voice was melodious and sounded sincere. Susan, looking up at his strongly-boned face, realised his twinkling brown eyes were melting her anger like the sun on ice. But she had no intention of forgetting his crime. She turned and frowned at the wreck of the balloon.

'Just look at the damage your giddy machine has done, sir.'

'What damage, ma'am? Ah, yes, it will cost me dearly to repair my flying machine. Silk costs a fortune, as well you know, ma'am.'

Of course Susan knew the cost of silk, but it was years since she'd owned a silk gown. At that moment she deeply regretted her clothes were not up to scratch, but why should she worry about her looks when he was half dressed! Seeing she was resisting his efforts to pacify her, Tom tried to explain.

'You must understand, ma'am, that until I can work out how to steer a balloon, it is at the mercy of the wind. I regret to say it's inclined to land where it will.'

He rejoiced to see his broad smile had succeeded in disarming her for a moment. He considered she should smile more often. Long lashes covered his eyes as he lowered them to view his lanky legs minus their breeches.

'As you can see, I did my best to keep it up by shedding all I could.' He gave a chuckle. 'And you must admit I was successful in avoiding your carriage.'

'It is no laughing matter, sir. You may have killed us!'

He scrutinised her scolding face thoughtfully. Indeed it would take a great deal to put down this little shrew! He coughed, using his hand to hide his grin.

'Life is, unfortunately, full of dangers, ma'am.'

Susan was becoming increasingly exasperated by the slippery manner in which he was refusing responsibility for his actions. Dashingly good-looking, dangerously charming and self-assured, he was also wildly irresponsible and fearless. Alas, so like her father had been — just the kind of man she should be avoiding.

But having stained her best shoes, and made an ass of herself over the sex of the cattle, and most of all finding herself prey to the sensual feelings he evoked, she was determined to gain something from her exertions. She would persevere until she at least received an apology from him.

'I think,' Susan said boldly, although quaking inside as she glared at the handsome flyer, 'you should, at least, apologise to my mama.'

Tom had the feeling he would not please her until he did. He bowed, hiding his smile.

'I will, of course, ma'am.'

Then he ran his fingers through his hair as he turned to look around.

'You will permit me to find some clothing first, eh?'

Susan frowned, annoyed by his teasing manner, although satisfied she'd won a partial victory. But she was not going to wait around for him to search for his garments. She would make her way back to the coach, cows or no cows!

Before she reached the gate, she became aware of the flyer striding after her so she quickened her pace, hoping to keep ahead of him. Alas, his long legs strode by her and he was there to open the gate, bowing — mockingly she suspected when she heard him chuckle — as she swept through.

What an infuriating man he was!

He'd managed to find his long waistcoat, which looked quaint over his underwear, but infinitely more presentable than before. Anyway why should she care how silly he looked? He accompanied her down the road in silence. Her chest ached because she could not breath easily with him striding beside her. He made her feel vulnerable and confused, and just when she was embarking on a fresh start in life and wanted to feel confident!

Oh, she knew it was her fault for allowing herself to be upset. Storming after him had been a mistake, and making him come to apologise. Now all she wanted was to be rid of him. She prayed he would apologise quickly, and they'd soon be on their way to Bath again, although, because of his antics, they'd arrive far later than she'd hoped.

On reaching the carriage, the coachman grinned to see the half-dressed flyer, but touched his forelock deferentially. Susan wondered whether the driver was too scared at the sight of such a commanding gentleman to dare complain. From the coach, Betty's voice could be heard.

'There, there, ma'am. Miss Susan will be back soon. Why, 'ere she is!'

Then Betty's voice became louder with excitement.

'She's with a tall gentle'um, ma'am, a right 'andsome fellow. Ooo! I think he be without 'is . . .'

Betty's voice trailed to a titter, and Lady Lavinia looked up sharply. Her distraught expression changed into a look of admiration.

'Why, sir, how very kind of you to

find my daughter.'

His state of undress did not seem to bother her ladyship in the slightest.

The flyer gave her a magnificent smile and a courtly bow. Susan watched in disbelief while he completely charmed her mama. The gallant way in which he lifted her mother's hand and kissed it made her flinch with anger. What a rogue he was, acting like a lord when he was nought but a reckless adventurer. But then Mama had a weakness for that kind of man. And Susan had to admire his polished manners which had instantly taken years off her mama, making her smile with his amusing small-talk.

They would be chit-chatting until nightfall! Susan interrupted them.

'Mama, this balloonist has only come to apologise for the fright he gave us.'

'But there is no need, sir,' Lady Lavinia assured him.

He shot Susan a triumphant smile, before turning to her mother again.

'I'm a scientist, ma'am, recently living

in Paris, where I was fortunate to observe the hot-air balloon built by the Montgolfier brothers, Joseph and Etienne, fly eight kilometres. That is five miles, ma'am.'

'That is most interesting, sir,' her ladyship murmured, as her lavender eyes sparkled under the warmth of his attention. 'Pray tell us more.'

'Mama! We really should be going now. It will be getting dark soon,' Susan interrupted them again, exasperated to find the crafty fellow would never apologise and they were being delayed for no purpose.

Lady Lavinia turned on her.

'Susan, dear, do mind your manners!'

Hearing the flyer chuckle, Susan felt tears come into her eyes. She took a long breath in as she pressed her lips together and tapped her foot impatiently. She was stunned to overhear her mother whispering confidentially to him.

'Do please forgive my daughter, sir. She has been well brought up, and is a darling. But she's recently lost her papa, and we are obliged to leave our home. It has been most distressing for her. However, she is quite right, we should continue our journey.'

Susan didn't know if she should laugh or cry seeing the glow on her mother's cheeks at having her authority restored by the charm of the attentive rogue.

'Betty,' Mama instructed, 'please tell the coachman we must be on our way.'

Susan suddenly felt a large warm hand take hers.

'May I help you into the coach?'

His voice had changed and he sounded concerned. His velvet brown eyes met hers. He looked kindly down at her for several moments. She battled to keep her wits when his hands clasped her tiny waist and she was lifted into the carriage as though she was no weight at all. She gave him a weak smile.

Ever since she'd met him he'd thrown her into a series of conflicting emotions. What an extraordinary situation. She'd been so cross with him, and yet now, as the carriage moved off, a small voice inside her was telling her that she didn't want to leave him! She'd been beguiled by the good-looking flyer, but not as much as Mama, who was now sitting contentedly with a little smile on her lips after announcing how delighted she was to have got away from London, and back into Bath's polite society.

Susan feared Bath would not be all pleasure for them. She gritted her teeth at the humiliating thought of being dependent. She decided she would do all she could to find a dependable gentleman who would be willing to marry her without a dowry. Of course, a gentleman like that might be a little dull. For some reason that flyer's devastating smile would not leave her memory. He was not in the least dull.

But never would she allow herself to become besotted by a reckless man as her dear mama had done. Papa had been a charming, but irresponsible man. All he had done for Mama was to gradually gamble away her considerable dowry, and leave his family to face an uncertain future.

As the miles went by, Mama dozed, and Susan, looking out of the carriage window, noticed it was becoming dusk. She also noticed they were passing tall houses. Clasping her hands tightly together she realised somewhat nervously that they were entering the famous City of Bath.

2

It was after their coach had driven out of sight that Tom suddenly remembered a begging letter his steward had told him about — some distant relatives needing accommodation. He'd only just returned from France and was only half-listening as there had been so many concerns for him to attend to. Tomorrow, when he saw his steward, Mr Berry, he'd have to ask him what arrangements he'd made for them.

Then he spied his wagon coming to collect him and his balloon. He considered he'd enjoyed a successful flight today, his longest time in the air, over ten miles he reckoned. So why was he feeling a little perturbed?

As he directed his men to find his belongings which were scattered around the fields he tried to concentrate his mind on the scientific results of the flight. But what kept cropping up in his mind was that he'd neglected to find out where Susan was going to live. In fact, he didn't even know her surname.

He'd found her most attractive. She was the kind of spirited, young woman he liked, and since her mama had told him of her father's death, he'd felt the greatest sympathy for her, as he, too, had recently lost his beloved father.

It explained her prickliness. Of course he'd been teasing her, and now he regretted he'd treated her so shabbily, although she was a determined little madam!

Although plainly dressed, she was obviously a gentlewoman. It was possible she might appear at the Bath Assembly Rooms. He gave a sigh. It was not his habit to frequent that establishment. He preferred to avoid the indiscreet husband-hunting matrons with their simpering daughters in tow, but for a night or two he would go and hope to find her there. Just why he wanted to find her he was not sure.

Meanwhile, unsure of the best route to their new home in Bath, the coachman was taking the ladies around the street of the fashionable spa. The stone buildings glowed a honey colour in the early evening light.

Lady Lavinia had remained in the best of spirits since making the acquaintance of the balloonist. Her excitement at being back in the city she remembered from her happy childhood was caught by her daughter, who listened attentively to her mama's commentary as they were being driven around.

'Notice the flagstoned promenades. They were made to allow the very wide hooped skirts we wore when we were young to be shown at their best advantage.'

Susan turned her head to watch a well-dressed couple taking a stroll. She didn't feel ill-mannered to stare as the couple were obviously out to display themselves.

'They have built so much more here

since I was a girl,' Mama chattered on, 'but I recognise this part. Now we are coming into the King's Circus. It is said Mr Wood got the idea from a circle of buildings from the Coliseum in Rome. Isn't it magnificent?'

Susan's anxieties were temporarily forgotten as she admired the beauty of the curving, terrace buildings with their elegant, classical proportions.

'Ho, there!' the coachman called, reining in the horses and attracting the attention of a pie seller.

After asking the way, the coach was turned and they were trundled down Gay Street, and passed Queen's Spare.

'I remember this lovely square, too,' Lady Lavinia cried as her eyes sparkled. 'I can't wait to see the shops!'

Susan smiled sadly. Lovely shops there might be in Bath, but money to spend in them was a different matter.

By now, the lamplighters were busy illuminating the darkening city. Like stage lights beaming on the drawn curtains in a theatre, the street lights created the setting for what was to come. There were not many of the Quality about. Dinner was over and most were dressing for the night's entertainment.

The Assembly Rooms would soon open. Parties, plays and concerts would begin. Sedan chairmen were already taking orders from the servants of socialites to carry their masters and mistresses through the streets to their chosen destination.

Susan drew in a lengthy breath. Despite her apprehension about the frugal life ahead of her, she was most impressed by what she'd seen of the unique city, and felt a sudden thrill knowing that the next stage of her life was about to begin here.

She looked out of the window anxiously as the carriage drew to a halt in front of a modest row of terraced houses in Milsom Street. Her heart beat faster when she recognised the number of the house the steward had given her.

'I'm well pleased if this is to be our

little home,' Lady Lavinia declared clapping her gloved hands together. 'It looks just perfect.'

Susan's eyes, however, noticed several things her mama had missed. One was that the house appeared to be already occupied. Candlelight shone from the curtained windows on the first floor. It was not going to be their house entirely. Also there were signs of workmen there. Pots of paint, planks of wood, and piles of wood chippings lay around the front door.

After ringing the doorbell, the coachmen drove off, leaving the travel-weary ladies, with their maid, standing on the pavement surrounded by their few belongings.

'There is no servant answering the bell,' Susan said. 'Shall we go in?'

'Betty you stay here and guard our luggage,' her ladyship instructed as she followed her daughter into the dimly-lit hall.

'Susan, I can't see at all well. Can't you light a candle?

There was no need. A light had suddenly appeared at the top of the flight of stairs.

An impressive lady in black holding a branch of flickering candles appeared, and called down to them in a genteel voice.

'You must be Lady Lavinia and Miss Woodford.'

Before Susan or her mother could reply, the lady began to sweep down the steps saying, 'Welcome to Bath, my dears. I expect you are tired and would like a dish of tea before I show you your rooms?'

Susan gave a curtsey and smiled gratefully.

'Thank you, ma'am.'

Mama did not bow to the kindly lady but grasped her daughter's arm whispering, 'Did she say we shall only have rooms here?'

'Yes, Mama,' Susan whispered back, her cheeks flaming seeing her mother's frostiness. 'It's quite common for people to share a house, here in Bath anyway,' she said soothingly, hoping to avoid disagreement.

There were times when Mama's aristocratic air was embarrassing. Why couldn't Mama remember they were in no position to make demands? Susan turned to the lady.

'Mama has been unwell, and this has been a most tiring journey for her,' she said.

To Susan's relief, the lady did not appear in the least put out by her mother's haughtiness. She nodded and smiled.

'The downstairs rooms are being altered to accommodate you, Lady Lavinia. As you can see, the carpenters are still working on them, but they assure me they will finish tomorrow. Now, do allow me to escort you upstairs to my parlour. I feel sure you'll be able to cope with your unpacking all the better if you are refreshed.'

'Very well, we shall take tea first,' Lady Lavinia conceded and walked over to the stairs, but before she took one step up she stopped. 'What about Betty?' she inquired imperiously.

'Betty is her maid,' Susan explained hurriedly. 'The girl is waiting outside on the pavement with our luggage.'

'Oh, then I will call Patrick to rescue your maid, and your luggage.'

The lady walked over to tug a bell rope. Moments later, a tiny woman shuffled from the back of the house wiping her hands on her long apron. She bobbed seeing the ladies in the hall.

'Sure, I didn't answer the bell,' she began in her Irish lilt before anything was said to her. 'Me hands were in the pastry dough, so they were. I thought Patrick would answer the door, but heaven knows where he is, your ladyship.'

So this graceful lady was an aristocrat, too! Susan wondered why such a fine lady should be living in this small house, and have such an odd servant. But then was not her mother in the same position?

'Annie,' the lady said, 'the ladies'

maid is outside. Please bring her in, and tell Patrick to collect their luggage.'

'I will, ma'am.'

'Annie, we shall take tea in my parlour now, and have supper later.'

'Very good, ma'am,' Annie said obligingly before trotting off.

As they climbed the stairs, Lady Lavinia inquired, 'May we know your name?'

'Why, I am Lady Mary.'

Recognising her to be the earl's sister, whom she had never met, Lady Lavinia now had nothing to feel superior about.

The parlour they were shown into was attractive with blue and pink flowered Chinese wallpaper, which gave the small room a pleasant airiness. Many items of the finest porcelain were on display, and Susan recognised the furniture as Chippendale's Chinese pieces.

'What a charming room this is!'

'Why thank you, Miss Woodford. Pray be seated.'

Gliding over to her rosewood tea

table, Lady Mary lit the burner under the tea urn.

'I must explain,' she said. 'I only knew of your coming a few days ago. The earl has been abroad until quite recently and when his steward told me that he had been given instructions to find you lodgings immediately, why I could only think that you may find it comfortable living here with me.'

'How very kind,' said Lady Lavinia, and Susan felt overjoyed to see her mother begin to chat pleasantly with her hostess.

Sipping her hot tea, Susan glanced around the parlour which appeared a little overcrowded with furniture and ornaments. The thought struck her that some things had probably been moved up from downstairs rooms. And although agreeing with her mother that Lady Mary was most kind, she did wonder if there was a reason for such generosity. But she felt sure it was for no evil reason. Lady Mary was not only charming but displayed elegance and grace.

Looking at her, Susan decided that if she observed her deportment and manners carefully she might learn a great deal of social expertise, which would assist her in her quest for a worthy gentleman to marry. Susan gave a contented sigh. They had arrived safely in Bath, and the future did not seem bad at all.

* * *

After tea, when they went downstairs to view their spacious reception room at the front of the house, Lady Lavinia exclaimed, 'This room is delightful! With two large sash windows it will provide excellent light. And I do like the sand-coloured walls trimmed in pale cream.'

'I'll get Patrick to help you to arrange the furniture as you wish it,' Lady Mary said.

Next to the sitting-room was another fair-sized room, painted blue on the walls and with white wainscoting. Fresh-looking and clean, it was to be Lady Lavinia's bedchamber. Susan watched as her mama sank down gratefully on to the floral embroidered counterpane covering the feather bed.

'Perhaps Mama could have her supper on a tray in her room this evening, Lady Mary. She is tired out.'

'Of course she shall, Miss Woodford. In fact it might be best for you as well this evening because I expect you are tired, too.'

'Oh, yes indeed, ma'am, thank you.'

Susan's room was adjoining and much smaller, but it had pretty chintz drapes over the bed, on the chair, and around the window. There was a dressing-table, a cheval-glass, as well as a wash stand with a decorated pitcher and washbowl.

'Why this is the prettiest bedchamber I've ever had!' Susan exclaimed.

'When it is light you will be able to see the garden from the window and the church steeple over the garden wall,'

Lady Mary said.

Patrick, the size of an Irish leprechaun with a cheeky grin, humped in their luggage.

Delighted with the modest, but adequate arrangements made for them, Susan was also pleased to see Betty looking happy when she popped in later having helped Lady Lavinia to unpack and undress into her nightcap and gown.

'Your mama enjoyed her supper, miss,' the maid reported, 'and I did, too. Annie's a good cook,' she said licking her lips. 'Now before I goes to leap on to me flea pallet, is there anything I can 'elp you wif?'

'No, thank you, Betty. I can manage to put my few things away.' But then Susan noticed Betty's reluctance to leave her, and enquired, 'Is there anything the matter?'

'You'd never guess what Annie told me.'

Susan could tell the young maid was longing to tell her, so she said as she picked up a gown from her trunk and shook it, 'Go on tell me.'

'Annie said your uncle, Lord Richard Dearham, be dead. There be a new earl now.'

Horror made Susan feel as if a large spider was running down her neck. What right had she and her mama to expect any assistance from a new Lord Dearham? She knew her uncle had married again after Mama's sister had died, but she knew nothing of the heir.

'Have you told Lady Lavinia?' she asked hoarsely.

'Lordy miss, 'course I didn't.'

Wild thoughts ran around Susan's head as she clung hold of the dressing-table for support. She had requested charity from a man she didn't know! Now she might be accused of stealing under false pretences and sent to gaol! The error must be confessed straight away. She took in a shuddering breath.

'Go to bed, Betty, but before you do, ask Patrick to meet me in the hall in ten minutes.'

When Betty had left the room Susan hastily scribbled a note for the Earl of Dearham. Then she found Patrick and asked him to have it delivered to his lordship that very evening, and reluctantly parted with her last guinea to have it sent by messenger.

Feeling mentally tied in knots trying to think how she and Mama could avoid landing up in the poorhouse, Susan went to bed, and being exhausted, she soon fell asleep.

Bright morning sunlight filled her bedchamber. Half-awake Susan snuggled comfortably under her bedclothes listening to doves cooing outside, instead of London's traffic and the shouts and sing-songs of the street vendors. Mama could be heard snoring gently next door and so she felt in no hurry to get up. A tap on her chamber door made Susan rise on one elbow.

'Yes?'

Betty poked her head around the door.

'Lord Dearham is 'ere to see you, miss,' she said softly.

Alarmed that a peer of the realm had come so early, and must therefore be irate, Susan leaped out of bed and sped to the wash-stand to splash water over her face. She then slipped on a simple morning gown and pinned her hair neatly under her cap.

Before leaving her bedchamber, she glanced in the mirror. She hoped to give the impression that she was a girl in need, and had not intended to deceive his lordship. She took a long breath in. If there was a time she needed to be brave it was certainly now.

There was no grandee waiting in the hall for her, only a workman busy putting up some wall lights in the front room. She was just wondering where Lord Dearham could be when she heard a guffaw of male laughter coming from Lady Mary's parlour. So he was upstairs.

Feeling in a quandary, Susan frowned. She knew if she waited for him to come downstairs, Mama might wake up. And it might be preferable if Mama was not around when she confronted his lordship. Bracing herself, she lifted her skirts and stepped resolutely upstairs and knocked on Lady Mary's parlour door.

'Come in,' she heard Lady Mary call.

Seized by a sudden shakiness, Susan found she could not move. Male footsteps could be heard pounding across the room. The door was flung open and a tall gentleman blocked the doorway. Susan's hand went to her mouth in amazement when their eyes met. His handsome face was familiar. He was the balloonist she'd met yesterday!

Struggling to recover her composure she stuttered, 'Oh, I beg your pardon. I was looking for someone else.'

His fine eyes glinted, and a quirky smile lifted the corners of his mouth.

'No, there is no mistake. I came to see you, Miss Woodford.'

His seductive voice played havoc

with her senses.

'But you can't be . . .'

'Yes, I am Dearham.'

Faintness made her head spin. Surely this irresponsible, young man couldn't be the new Earl of Dearham, to whom she must explain that she and her mother were in dire need!

From inside the parlour, Lady Mary called, 'Tom, pray do not conduct your conversation on the landing. Let Miss Woodford in. I shall go and finish my toilet.'

Before Susan could find anything to say, Lord Dearham had stepped aside so that his aunt could pass out of the room. She said a pleasant, 'Good morning,' to Susan as she rustled by in her black silk gown, leaving a delightful perfume behind as she swished away along the corridor.

'Do come in, Miss Woodford.'

Susan had to summon all her courage to enter the room and, hearing the door being closed behind her, she almost panicked. How superb he looked in his impeccable riding clothes, every inch a lord. His assurance was noticeable — but this morning Susan wished he would not glare at her so. He seemed bigger and more powerful than ever as he towered over her.

'I received your missive last night saying you must see me urgently. Well, ma'am, I have come. Now, what have you to say?' he said.

Alas, the words in her note, written in haste last night when she was tired, were a trifle dictatorial in the fresh light of the morning.

'Sir, I did not mean — '

'Then please be quick and explain what you did mean. I happen to have several pressing engagements today. Having to come into town this morning especially to see you has been most inconvenient.'

He was making her nervous — unable to think straight. She was annoyed to hear him raise his voice. It was not her fault that this misunderstanding about her uncle had arisen.

'Miss Woodford,' he said with an exasperated sigh when she stood struggling for the right words, 'you were vocal enough with me yesterday, so why this coyness today, eh?'

Suddenly her temper completely obliterated her resolve to apologise. She lifted her chin, determined to show him he could not crush her.

'Lord Dearham,' she said icily, 'there's no need for you to be uncivil.'

'Uncivil?' he cried striking his fist down on the table making the lustre ornament jump.

His wild behaviour made Susan step backwards. She knew she was completely at his mercy and should control her temper.

'My lord, forgive me, it was quite wrong of me to have criticised you just now.'

'You have done nothing but criticise me ever since I met you! You are extremely rude, madam.'

Rude! Hurt burned her face red. So that is what he thought of her!

'And you, sir, are unfeeling!'
He almost choked.
'Me? Unfeeling?'
'Yes indeed,' she said boldly, delighted to see him taken aback. 'I had no wish to inconvenience you when I wrote to you last night, but I had just learned that my uncle had died, something I did not know when I wrote to the Earl of Dearham for assistance.'
As he regarded her thoughtfully, she added, 'I don't want to be a dependant. But I had to find somewhere for Mama to live. As for myself, I plan to marry a respectable gentleman with means as soon as it is at all possible.'
'Alas, ma'am, I can't think of a single respectable gentleman who would take you on. It would be more than his life's worth!'
His face came to within inches of hers, but she stood her ground. She could not retort that no female would want to marry him, for he was far too good-looking, and charming when he wanted to be.

Seeing her at a loss for words, he grinned and said, 'But, coming to think on it, I dare say a retired army man might suit you.'

Tears welled in her eyes. The thought of having to marry a wealthy but portly colonel, or a hard-faced captain, or even a squire with gout she had to push around in a bath chair appalled her.

'I fear you may be right,' she said sadly.

Now it was Lord Dearham's turn to falter. Seeing her burning cheeks he felt ashamed of himself taunting the poor girl. The clock on the mantelpiece chimed and, scraping his hair back from his forehead with his fingers, he came closer and looked deeply into her glassy eyes.

'Miss Woodford,' he said softly, 'I shall be happy to assist you and your mama. You have my word on it. But I must leave now as I'm already late for an important engagement.'

As he went to pick up his beaver hat and crop, he noticed the tears trickling down Susan's cheeks and felt horrified. His father, the late earl, had always tried to drum into him the necessity of being courteous to those less fortunate than himself. And what a mess he'd made of this interview! But he had no time to make matters right now. He bowed.

'My Aunt Mary is coming to Dearham Hall tomorrow for dinner. Will you and your mother accompany her, and then we can discuss this matter further, eh?' he said.

'Thank you, my lord,' she replied and curtsied.

He strode to the door and then turned to her.

'Good day to you, Miss Woodford. Please give my best wishes to Lady Lavinia.'

When he'd left the parlour she heard him call out, 'Goodbye, Mary, my love. I must run. I look forward to seeing you, with Lady Lavinia and Miss Woodford at dinner tomorrow.'

She heard him clatter down the stairs two at a time, march across the hall and let himself out of the front door. Something drew her to the window to watch him untether his fine horse, and leap on to its back. Then, wheeling the animal around with a clatter of hooves, he rode off out of sight.

What a confused mixing of anger, embarrassment and a longing to see him again she felt!

3

Susan hurriedly wiped her eyes when she heard Lady Mary enter the room. Quickly, she composed herself.

'Oh dear me, Miss Woodford, I regret Tom has upset you!'

'He,' Susan mumbled while dabbing her eyes, 'was a little cross with me for having inconvenienced him, that is all.'

'I should explain Lord Dearham is really a very kind, young man, although he can have occasional bouts of ill humour which are soon over, and best forgotten. Now do sit down, Miss Woodford. I don't suppose you've had any breakfast. Shall we have some together?

When Susan gave her a weak smile and nodded in agreement, Lady Mary sailed over and pulled the bell rope before coming to sit down gracefully beside her. Susan's voice trembled a little when she spoke.

'Ma'am, I should have noticed your were in mourning. I didn't know my uncle had died until last night.'

'Don't let it worry you, my dear.'

Feeling Lady Mary was an understanding person she could confide in, Susan explained.

'I expect you know I had written to my uncle to beg him for help as my father gambled away all his money, and all our possessions. We are without funds.'

Lady Mary leaned forward and patted Susan's hand.

'So I understand. But the new earl is happy to provide for you. He is immensely rich.'

'But Mama and I have taken your rooms downstairs!'

'My dear, the truth is I'm glad to have your company in the house. I lost my dear husband several years ago, and now my brother, Richard, has gone, so it will be pleasant for me to have yours and Lady Lavinia's company here.'

Susan smiled gratefully at her elegant companion. A tap on the door heralded Annie who carried in a breakfast tray. The maid was asked to bring an extra cup for the young lady, which she did. Sipping her hot chocolate, Susan decided to broach the last of her worries.

'Lady Mary, I need to get married.'

'Of course, and I expect you'll soon have many admirers here in Bath to choose from. I think Tom is quite taken with you.'

Susan went pink.

'Oh, no, he doesn't like me at all!'

She didn't want to say she didn't have in mind a reckless flying adventurer like Lord Dearham.

'Do you think it will be difficult for me to find a respectable, trustworthy gentleman here — a clergyman or an army officer perhaps?'

Lady Mary trilled, 'I don't think you should do more than look for someone to love, which wouldn't be difficult as I think you have every asset a woman could want. You are an agreeable size and move well, your voice is clear and well pitched. You have lovely hair and a complexion many girls would envy.'

Elated, Susan's eyes sparkled at Lady Mary. Then her face fell.

'But I have no suitable clothes to wear in this fashionable city.'

'Indeed, clothes are most important. But before you enter society, we shall see about that, too. I have one or two gowns my dressmaker can alter to suit you.'

Second-hand clothes were not ideal but Susan felt like hugging her. All her worries seemed to be at an end.

'Oh, thank you, Lady Mary, you've made me happy.'

'And so you should be at your age. I think you've had too much sorrow to bear, but now you shall enjoy being here. And tomorrow we are to visit Dearham Hall. Richard built the fine country house. I'm sure you and your mama will enjoy seeing where his son now lives.'

'Yes,' Susan agreed but her smile had vanished.

She wasn't looking forward to meeting the overpowering young Lord Dearham again.

* * *

During the carriage drive to Dearham Hall, Susan felt thrilled to see the countryside again and looked around at the scenery as her mama and Lady Mary chatted. When Dearham Hall came into view she was enchanted. The Palladian-style mansion built in the sandy-coloured Bath freestone was magnificent. The park trees were newly planted but in years to come they would grow and flourish.

A liveried footman approached to open the carriage door when they arrived at the entrance, he made an announcement.

'His lordship asked me to tell you that he is in the stable paddock, ma'am, but will join you later for dinner.'

Lady Mary turned to the ladies.

'Tom is occupied with his scientific experiments I expect. He will want us to make ourselves at home, so come in, my dears, and I will show you around.'

Lady Lavinia was delighted, but Susan, knowing Lord Dearham had asked her to come because he wanted to discuss her situation, decided the sooner the interview was over the better.

'Lady Mary I should like a quick word with his lordship before dinner,' she said.

'Very well. Why don't you stay in the coach and you will be taken to the stables?'

Susan's heart began to thud as the horses clattered into the cobbled courtyard and she saw the rows of stables, but no sign of Lord Dearham. As she stood perplexed she heard a man's footsteps behind her and turned to see an exquisitely-dressed gentleman approaching her.

'Bonjour, mademoiselle.'

He gave Susan a charming smile and

an elaborate bow. Anyone would think she was wearing silks and satins instead of a well-worn, ordinary-looking cotton gown.

'Good day sir. I'm looking for Lord Dearham. Do you know where he is?' she inquired.

His bright eyes were appraising her as he most courteously offered her his arm.

'I am going to find him myself. I shall show you, ma chèrie.'

As he walked her towards a far gate he said, 'You are a lady friend of his, n'est-ce-pas?

'No, sir, I am not.'

He smiled.

'Then you will be mine, eh?'

Susan stiffened at the thought. She did not know this Frenchman, but felt he was too forward and wanted to pull her arm away. And yet the thought struck her that if she wanted to meet and marry a respectable gentleman she would have to learn to be more friendly towards men. Before she had time to analyse her feelings further, they arrived at the paddock to see a bizarre scene. Susan blinked and stared.

The great balloon's envelope was spread across the sunlit grass, and working on it, like Gulliver's little people, were several men, boys and women. Patches were being sewn over the tears in the yellow and orange silk. The netting was being mended. Long lengths of willow were soaking in a horse trough, and some were being woven to repair the damage to the balloon's basket.

In charge of them all was Lord Dearham. Susan's stomach churned to see how strong and healthily attractive he looked in an open-necked shirt with country-style breeches.

Seeing them, his lordship flicked back his tousled hair from his eyes and called in his deep voice, 'Where have you been, Jean-Paul? Come here, I need your advice.'

Jean-Paul murmured, 'Forgive me, mademoiselle, I must leave you,' and went to join his lordship.

Affronted to be ignored, Susan watched the two men converse, but before she could decide what to do, she spied Lord Dearham's lofty figure heading towards her. She had the feeling his dark eyes were staring right into her soul. There was no escape, so although quaking more the closer he came, she tried not to show it.

This was not going to be the quiet, private meeting with him she had envisaged. But before his lordship came nearer, his attention was diverted by a call from one of the women working on the netting. He changed direction and crouched down to view her work. Turning his head he called out towards Susan.

'Help us over here, if you please, Miss Woodford.'

She was no more than an extra pair of hands! But laughing, she lined up with the other women while Lord Dearham used his great strength to tug the netting out flat. Then he got the women to hold it up while he carefully inspected their repair work.

'Excellent!' he announced joyfully. 'Here's a shilling each for your fine threading.'

Emptying his pocket he handed a coin to each cooing woman.

Devilishly, Susan chirped, 'Don't I get one, too, sir? Work without pay don't butter no parsnips!'

Tossing the rest of the coins in the air and catching them in his large hand he pocketed them saying, 'You haven't done much to help.'

Which was true, of course. But she was only funning. She gave a scornful little laugh and said, 'I only came to speak to you, not to waste my time with this trivia!'

She heard him hiss in his breath. His sharp glare made her cringe while his fine, aristocratic nostrils flared and in a deadly quiet voice he asked, 'Have I done something wrong again, Miss Woodford?'

Susan stifled an urge to scream at him

when she heard the women giggle. Shaking with rage she used both hands to grasp her skirts high so that she could walk away quickly.

Tom forgot his project for a few minutes as he watched her retreat, uncomfortably aware that his gaze was hypnotically drawn to her nubile figure admirably shown in her plain, but attractive cotton gown. The bold toss of her head reminded him of a fiery Arab filly that needed breaking in, gently of course, so that the animal's spirit was not broken.

He gave a loud sigh. Once more he had been guilty of losing his temper with her. He couldn't understand it. Normally ladies responded well to him, but Susan Woodford was entirely different. She was quite the most tantalising and intriguing woman he'd ever come across. He swore to himself.

Much as he wanted to see his balloon's repairs finished and ready for launch, he knew he ought to go and repair the damage he'd done to Miss

Woodford's dignity first.

Entering the house, Susan hoped her eyes did not look red and watery. Her face was still hot, but she hoped that by the time she found Lady Mary and her mama it would have cooled down. It was too bad that instead of improving her standing with Lord Dearham she had created another storm, or was it his fault this time?

A footman showed her into the grand hall and as she walked up the wide stone staircase the pleasing interior had a soothing effect on her. By the time she entered the cream and gilt drawing-room and saw the two ladies sitting by the long sash windows looking out over the parkland she was able to return their welcoming smiles.

'Did you find Tom?' Lady Mary asked.

'Yes, I saw him, but he was so occupied with his toy balloon I did not have the chance to talk to him.'

Lady Mary gave her a rueful smile.

'I should have warned you, my dear

Miss Woodford. He has a scientific mind. Yes, I'm afraid when he is concentrating on his experiments everything else might well not exist. His father was the same.'

Susan sank down on a chair near her mother and was pleased to see how content Mama looked. At least one of them was benefiting from their visit to Dearham Hall.

Lady Mary said, 'It will soon be time for dinner then you will have the chance to speak to him again. Now shall I show you the library, my dears?'

It was indeed a fine collection of books, and Susan was so engrossed in looking around that she didn't notice the ladies walking out to view the hot-houses. The sound of bold footsteps coming towards her made her realise it could only be one person. His lordship was coming into the library! She was trapped.

In a panic, she seized a book from the shelves and sat down on a library chair. Perhaps if she remained still he wouldn't see her. Her chest heaved. Why was it that she could cope with London's rough Covent Garden traders, but this ill-tempered earl made her behave like a furtive child?

'Ah, so there you are, Miss Woodford!'

As she gave a startled jump, the book slipped from her lap and fell to the floor. He swooped to pick it up and glancing at the title on the spine, his handsome face smiled as he returned it to her.

Irritated to hear him chuckle, she said, 'Am I making myself a nuisance again, my lord, by reading one of your books?'

'Indeed, no.'

Pretending to be more interested in the book than him, Susan remarked, 'Then are you amused to find that I can read and write?'

'I just didn't know you were a scholar, Miss Woodford.'

'I'm not,' she snapped, but looking down again at the book she found it was printed in Greek!

In a disgraceful lack of self-control, she gave a shrill cry of frustration and threw it straight at him!

'Ouch!'

It hit him on the elbow as he has raised his arm to protect his face. Alarm smote her as she realised she'd struck her benefactor.

To her relief he laughed.

'You're a capital shot, ma'am!'

He rubbed his elbow ruefully.

'I think I'd better get out of here as there are far too many books for you to throw at me!'

After she'd returned the book to its shelf, she turned to find him blocking her way.

'Ma'am, I owe you an apology.'

Susan's eyes widened. She really ought to apologise to him. The more she was with this man the more confused he made her. She cleared her throat.

'Sir, I find you impossible to comprehend.'

'And I have never come across a young lady quite as contrary.'

As she looked up into his eyes she found he did not seem really cross with her. Feeling a blush rise, she drew in a long breath.

'Lord Dearham, I am a perfectly normal woman.'

'We shall see, shall we?'

She stiffened as she felt his hand slide around her waist drawing her towards him. He bent his head and his lips came nearer, firm yet pliant lips that threatened to land on hers! She gave a little gasp, but like a wanton creature, she could not bring herself to draw her head away. He was bewitching her into kissing him.

It seemed natural to place her hands around his neck, to feel his strong arms glide around her slender body. The sweet bliss of his kiss sent dazzling stabs of excitement through her and for a moment she felt she never wanted to part from him.

Remorse suddenly swept over her. Drawing away for him she said, 'You need not demonstrate your reckless, rakish behaviour on me, sir.'

He looked flabbergasted.

'Who told you I was a rake?'

'It is obvious you take advantage of unprotected women.'

He gave a low whistle.

'Miss Woodford, I wonder at your pointing an accusing finger at me. The way you react in a man's arms it is a wonder you are allowed to go unchaperoned!'

Cheeks flaming, Susan stammered, 'I . . . I . . . b . . . . beg your pardon?'

He pushed his hair off his forehead, but it fell back again.

'Well, ma'am, you hardly hung back when I kissed you just now.'

Susan's bosom rose and fell as she glared at him. She wanted to tell him exactly what she thought of him, but she dare not, not while she and her mama were dependent upon his charity. It would just have to wait until the day she had secured a respectable husband. She darted away from him before she said anything she might later regret. She was thankful he made no effort to chase her.

As she went to join the ladies, however, she realised her heart was singing. Lord Dearham had kissed her! She'd enjoyed it. Her lips still felt delightfully warm. Then a little groan escaped her lips. She'd discovered how easy it was to be carried away by passion and she would have to control her feelings. Ardour did not fit into her scheme of finding a man with a good reputation to marry.

Meanwhile, Tom stood in his library with a perturbed expression on his face. Miss Woodford was causing him more mental disturbance than enough, although he'd found her exquisite to kiss. She was indeed a passionate woman despite her plain-spoken manner. But when he should be thinking about the problems of flying again, before the winter weather set in, she was occupying his mind.

All he could think about was her beautiful eyes, her slender figure, and removing her cap so that he could run his fingers through her chestnut curls, and he longed to kiss her again!

Damnation! To forget her, he would go to London and amuse himself with friends for a few days, and when he returned, the balloon should be ready to launch.

4

Susan did not allow her differences with Lord Dearham to prevent her from enjoying her dinner at Dearham Hall. Sitting next to Jean-Paul, the elegantly-attired nephew of the famous Montgolfier brothers, whose hot-air balloon was the first to ascend into the heavens, she found his conversation most amusing. The more Jean-Paul told her about the art of ballooning, the more fascinated she became by it.

After the meal, the party went into the drawing-room for tea. As Lady Lavinia sat gossiping with Mr Berry, and Mary was presiding over the tea tray, Tom, tormented by Susan's soft laughter as she conversed with Jean-Paul, strolled over and sat next to his aunt.

'Aunt Mary,' he said quietly, 'I wish

to speak to you about Miss Woodford.'

Lady Mary's eyes flickered over to where Susan sat absorbed in Jean-Paul's prattling.

'She's such a pretty girl, don't you think?' she commented.

'I'm at my wits' end to know what to make of her,' the words growled out of him. 'She's driving me mad!'

'Don't be absurd, Tom. Here, hold this cup while I fill it.'

Mary lifted the china teapot and began to pour but noticed his lordship's hand was not as steady as it should be. She smiled knowingly. It was clear to her Tom was in love with the girl. Well, it was about time he settled down and got married.

'She has such a sweet nature, too!'

'Miss Woodford, sweet-natured? I think not. Why, she threw a book at me before dinner!'

Mary tittered.

'Did she now? You must have upset her.'

'Me? Upset her? Impossible, I'd say!'

'Well, she told me you called her rude.'

'And so she is. Mary, I shall be obliged if you will deal with her in future.'

'Deal with her? What do you mean?'

The young earl shook his head in exasperation. His aunt was a sympathetic woman, that was why he liked her. She'd practically been a mother to him since his mama had died years ago. But she did not seem to understand his dilemma.

He looked across to where Susan sat listening with rapt attention to Jean-Paul's amusing anecdotes. Now that Frenchman was a rake if ever there was one!

'Miss Woodford is headstrong and will get herself into trouble if she is not protected,' he said abruptly.

Susan, suddenly aware she was being scrutinised, looked up and stared over the room at Tom. Their eyes seemed to lock in combat. Aunt Mary frowned. Now she could see that there were certainly fireworks between those two young people she liked. She sighed. What a pity!

'Dearest Tom,' she said, 'you get on with your affairs. Miss Woodford has her own plans. She intends to go hunting for a husband and I intend to help her. Now would you be please, kind enough to take this cup of tea over to her?'

Good manners made his lordship rise obediently and take the cup although he would have preferred not to. As he crossed the room, he slid his long finger to loosen his stock which had suddenly seemed too tight around his neck, but in his heart he knew it was because he felt jealous seeing Jean-Paul dealing so well with the attractive, young lady. At the age of twenty-eight he should not be having difficulties on that score.

'Ah, my lord.'

Jean-Paul leaped to his feet, and taking the cup of tea from Tom, gave it to Susan with an exaggerated bow.

'I have asked Mademoiselle Woodford if she would like to take a ride in the great balloon with me. And she has said, yes, she would.'

Tom's mouth fell open. He glared at them both. How dare they arrange a flight without consulting him! But also, he was angry because the wretched woman had now begun to interfere with his private domain: ballooning. His lordship did not dare to say what was on his mind at that moment.

He would deal with Jean-Paul later, tell him in no uncertain manner that balloon flying was not an occupation for young ladies. He savagely brushed his hair back from his forehead, but checking his temper, he merely gave Susan a cutting look and stalked away.

Susan sat reeling. She'd only said she'd like to go up in a balloon lightly. She hadn't meant to be taken seriously! She could see Tom was angry about it, and as he was being kind and considerate to her and her mother, she wished she had not hurt him.

Looking for the opportunity to speak

to him and explain the misunderstanding, she was disappointed not to have the chance before they left Dearham Hall. It seemed to Susan that his lordship was trying to avoid her. He probably despised her!

Yet the way she'd noticed him look at her at times, steadily, penetratingly, did not look like hate. And she'd felt warm and safe in his arms when he kissed her.

I shall be especially nice to him the next time we meet, she decided.

Later, the Earl of Dearham paced the floor of his study. He knew Jean-Paul Montgolfier had every right to invite Miss Woodford to take a ride in the balloon. He was well aware that if it were not for Jean-Paul's expertise he would never have been able to construct the balloon, and the spectacular flights he'd enjoyed up in the heavens would not have occurred.

Flying, he realised, was still in its infancy, but was none the less exciting for that. However, it was a man's pastime because it could be dangerous.

Women should remain on the ground.

He looked round when his thoughts were interrupted as Jean-Paul came breezing in with the barest tap on the door. Tom grimaced to see the smug look on the Frenchman's face.

'Jean-Paul, aren't there enough petticoats on my estates without you dabbling with that Woodford female?'

'Oh, la-la!' Jean-Paul exclaimed. 'Is his lordship still a little out of sorts, eh?'

There were times when Tom wanted to throttle Monsieur Montgolfier! Jean-Paul lowered himself into a chair and took a tiny, ornate box from his jacket. Flicking open the lid with his fingernail, he pinched some snuff. With a flourish of the lace around his wrist, he placed the snuff under his nose and inhaled.

After sneezing, he said, 'Mademoiselle Woodford is très jolie, n'est pas?'

Normally, Tom liked Jean-Paul, and they worked well together. But he had to lay down the law at times.

'I grant you Miss Woodford has some

assets. Personally, I don't think she is worth pursuing. But I don't want you to either.'

'How unromantic you English are! You hunt the foxes, why not the girls?'

Tom's eyes narrowed. He suddenly felt the weight of the responsibilities he had taken over from his father, as though his carefree youth was at an end.

'Now look here, Jean-Paul. Miss Woodford is under my protection. I will not allow you to put her in any danger. However willing she is, you know I cannot allow her to fly.'

'But I promised her,' Jean-Paul said stubbornly. 'I only intend to take her up and then down again.'

Tom could detect the note of belligerence in Jean-Paul's voice. If he was not careful, this matter could turn into a full-blown row, which might lead the Frenchman to return to France and he would not be able to continue to fly without his scientific assistance.

'Oh, very well, Jean-Paul. I think it unwise, but I will allow you to take Miss

Woodford up for a few minutes so that she can see the view of the earth from the sky. But you are to keep the ropes on the balloon so it can't fly away. And afterwards you are to send her back to Bath and cast your amorous eyes elsewhere.'

'Bon!'

Jean-Paul leaped from his chair, satisfied his French pride was intact.

'I shall inform her when the weather is clement.'

He left the study backwards, bowing one of his courtly bows. Dismay hit Tom. He strode over to the window and slid it open, letting in a sharp blast of fresh air. Breathing deeply, he watched the gusty wind blowing the last of the leaves off the trees in the park and felt comforted that the weather was far too blustery for flying. He could go to London and forget about Jean-Paul and his madcap idea to take Miss Woodford flying.

As he slammed the window shut, it flashed into his mind that he would be glad to see Miss Woodford married and off his hands. He would send some guineas to Aunt Mary and ask her to dress the girl up and send her to the Assembly Rooms.

It was her idea anyway to find a husband. He stroked his chin. Perhaps a little encouragement in the form of a good dowry would also entice some gentleman to take her.

He stood wondering how much. One sum he thought of he then considered might be too much and would tempt a fortune hunter. But it had to be enough to attract a good man. Susan Woodford had her faults, but if he was honest with himself, he had to admit she had more than just physical attractions and would make some man a very presentable wife.

* * *

The following day, Aunt Mary showed Susan the secrets of her gilt, sweet-smelling boudoir, an array of lady's frippery Susan never dreamed existed.

Her closet contained some magnificent gowns, petticoats and shoes, as well as many other fashionable luxuries. Her collection of jewellery and embellished fans alone would be the envy of anyone aspiring to enter Society.

'Why all this lace and ribbons on the stays?' Susan asked. 'And the bows and frills, and expensive lace on an under-skirt?'

Then she blushed. Wasn't it obvious that beautiful underclothes were intended for a man to see! For some reason Susan recalled Lord Dearham's lips hovering over hers and recollected feeling no concern for modesty as she pressed her body to his. Oh dear, she felt confused. She had so much to learn!

She took a shaky breath in. She must forget him. Her quest was to find a tolerable, well-off man to marry. She reminded herself that her mama had married for love, and what a tragedy that had been!

Lady Mary showed her some of her gowns which Susan realised would be considered old-fashioned now.

'The actresses of the Comedie Italienne were the first to wear hooped skirts,' she explained showing a hoop frame joined together by stiff waxed cloth. 'They were laughed at for wearing them, but they soon became popular with fashionable women.'

'I should think these wide ones are uncomfortable to wear,' Susan remarked.

'Ah, but they look so feminine and elegant, my dear. That's what's important. You must be prepared to suffer for beauty. The main thing is to look attractive and catch a gentleman's eye because there will be many other pretty girls at the ball.'

But not many who will want the kind of man I'm after, Susan thought sadly.

'And you will need a good hairdresser as well as a skilled mantua maker, and I know of both,' Aunt Mary told her with twinkling eyes.

Susan fingered the luxurious materials and began to feel excited at the prospect of having some clothes of her own choice made with the money Lord Dearham had sent her that morning. She'd gone puce at first when she'd seen his note saying the gold was for her dress so that she could make her début. But such blatant charity had only made her more determined than ever to marry away from his largesse.

Looking around Bath's elegant shops was a great thrill for Susan. Both Mama and Lady Mary accompanied her. And Lady Mary of course knew where all the best shops were. As well as selecting her own materials and accessories, Susan purchased a new pair of kid gloves and shoes for Mama, and some lavender water for her, too. And Lady Mary suggested they stopped at a coffee shop for refreshment during their shopping expedition, so that frail Lady Lavinia could rest awhile.

When the day for Susan's début at the New Assembly Rooms in Bath arrived, she felt she'd been well prepared, but hearing that the Earl of Dearham had taken himself off to London was a disappointment. Having taken such care to present herself as a fashionable, young lady, having practised with Mama and Lady Mary how to walk, curtsey and dance gracefully in her new ball gown, she thought it a pity his lordship would not be there to see how she'd spent his money. Also, she felt sure he'd be a good dancer and would at least have requested one dance with her.

When she was dressed for the ball Lady Lavinia came in to see her daughter and exclaimed, 'You look quite beautiful in that oyster silk gown, my darling. The new higher waist style suits you admirably. Betty, tighten her sash a little, and let me adjust your ringlets. There now, you are going to look perfect when I've hung my pearls around your neck.'

'Oh, no, Mama! They are yours. You must wear them.'

'Susan, I have nothing else left to pass on to you when I die but these pearls. It would please me to see you wearing them, especially as you have no jewellery.'

Susan felt tears prick her eyes at her mother's thoughtfulness. And when Lady Mary saw her she agreed that the pearls sat well around her neck and enhanced her gown. Three sedan chairs were hired to carry the ladies to the Assembly Rooms. Betty, Annie and Patrick waved them off.

Sitting closeted in her chair Susan felt apprehensive. Bounced gently to the rhythm of the chairmen's footsteps, she looked out of the chair window to see the lamp-lit streets of Bath which gave a mysterious air. Indeed, the evening ahead was like a parcel to be unwrapped. She felt slightly fearful anticipating how her venture to find a husband would go. Then she reminded herself that she would not be the only marriageable female to be going there tonight with the same objective.

She thought it must be petrifying for

any shy girls straight out of the schoolroom to be paraded before the critical eye of the ton. At least she was attending because she chose to do so, and she had Lady Mary accompanying her, who was well acquainted with the patronesses, as well as Mama.

Bennett Street was crowded with fashionable folk eyeing each other as they paraded along, chatting excitedly, towards the Assembly Rooms. Although Susan had seen the building from the outside, it was going to be the first time she'd entered it and she was eager to see the interior.

The chairmen carried the sedan chairs around to the west entrance. They proceeded through three open double-doors which led them into a grand vestibule, lit by dozens of candles from a sparkling chandelier. As she emerged from her chair Susan was aware that fans stopped fluttering and eye-glasses were raised as she was scrutinised.

It took her some effort to smile and

appear unflustered as she accompanied the ladies swanning their way towards the crowded octagonal ante-chamber. Susan forced herself to ignore her pounding heart and remember her deportment. But as they entered the ballroom she stopped in dazed admiration at the dazzling sight.

Five enormous glittering chandeliers cast a flickering glow over the rows of dancers and those watching them, heightening the multi-coloured shimmering silks and deep velvet shadows.

Susan suddenly felt the urge to enter the magical atmosphere created by the orchestra and dancers, her feet practically aching to join in the minuet. Greeted by the Master of Ceremonies they were led to some vacant seats and joined the chaperones who could be seen nudging and asking about the newcomers.

Looking around at some of the girls forced to sit out as they had no dance partners, Susan was pleased to hear the words, 'May I have the honour of this dance, ma'am?'

She gladly accepted but was disappointed to find her partner was past his youth. He had a leathery face and she had to clench her teeth when her face came close to his during the dance because he had bad breath. Her next partner was rotund and a poor dancer, and she was not sorry when the dance came to an end. But as soon as the dance was over she found herself being prevented from returning to her seat by a bold gentleman blocking her way.

'Excuse me, sir,' she said trying to pass him, but when he refused to budge she raised her eye, and almost fainted.

She recognised Mr August Borman, the hard-faced London creditor!

'So I have netted you, my slippery fish!' he rasped. 'We have some unfinished business. Come with me.'

Gasping for breath, Susan thought quickly. She did not want to create a scene here in this elegant assembly, nor did she want Mama to see him. Better to allow herself to be escorted out of the crowded ballroom and then she would attempt to extract herself from his grip.

Dragged outside by an iron fist clamped around her delicate wrist, August Borman stopped in the empty corridor and sneered at her.

'So you thought you could run off with some of your father's money that now belongs to me, did you, Miss Woodford?'

Her mouth dry, Susan tried not to panic.

She said as calmly as she could, 'No sir. You took all my father's money, our house, the horses and carriages, everything.'

'I think not. You look far from being in the poorhouse, my dear. I see you have the money to dress yourself up in silk and attend this fine assembly.'

Fear made Susan dumb as she saw the mean glint in his eyes. His rough fingers encircled Mama's pearls.

'These baubles belong to me, unless . . . ' He glared down at her cleavage and then smirked into her horrified eyes. 'Unless you are willing to be my mistress.'

A chill ran down her spine as despair engulfed her. Suddenly someone grasped her waist and swung her away from her tormentor. Turning, she saw a broad-shouldered figure land a mighty blow on August Borman's nose, sending him sprawling on the floor with a yowl of pain.

'Sir,' a commanding voice she recognised boomed, 'apologise to this lady and leave this instant, or I shall be obliged to throw you out!'

Relief at having the Earl of Dearham come to her rescue made her weak-kneed. She leaned against the wall and watched Mr Borman grovelling on the floor, his bloodied face distorted with pain.

'Apologies, Miss Woodford,' he muttered before being hauled to his feet by the earl's strong hand on his coat.

Without releasing his quarry, his lordship dictated, 'If there is anything to settle in the late Mr Woodford's affairs, which I doubt, you will see my steward, Mr Berry. Now get out and be warned. If you make any further attempt to contact Lady Lavinia or her daughter, you will have me to deal with.'

Susan watched with relief as the loathsome creditor lurched away down the corridor. She took a deep breath and looking up at her saviour said shakily, 'Thank you, my lord.'

'You should have told me about him.'

Susan prevented herself from saying that trying to tell him anything was almost impossible. His bearing, his perfectly-cut dark suit on his splendid physique made her feel unworthy of his company. It also occurred to her how disappointed he must feel to have found her in difficulties.

'I'm sorry,' she said. 'I didn't expect to find Mr Borman here in Bath. Nor did I expect to see you, my lord. I thought you were in London.'

His face softened and she longed to lay her aching head on his broad shoulder, and for him to put his arms around her and comfort her.

'Come,' he said offering her his arm, 'forget Mr Borman. That depraved bully will not be bothering you again. Now, I promised Aunt Mary that I would dance with you at your come-out. Do you feel recovered enough to do me the honour?'

Feeling shaky still, Susan felt she wanted to go home, but looking up at the sympathetic expression on his lordship's face she knew he was being kind. And what better man could restore her self-confidence than Lord Dearham who was the epitome of self-assurance?

'Yes, thank you, I will,' she said, endeavouring to cast aside the disastrous start to the evening and begin afresh with him.

Taking his arm, she looked up and gave him a radiant smile. His devastating smile in return sent shivers of joy through her, and when he lowered his head to give her the lightest kiss, and whispered, 'Well done, ma'am,' as if he knew she'd had a struggle to compose herself again, she rejoiced at the better understanding between them.

5

Dancing with Lord Dearham sent Susan's mind and heart soaring to heaven. He was the perfect partner, dancing superbly. After refreshments he danced with her again, and again, so that Susan felt she wanted the bliss to last for ever.

Not that she didn't partner some other pleasant, young men during the evening, but Lord Dearham was by far the most outstanding gentleman in the room. And for Susan he was her champion because he had rescued her from Mr Borman, and restored her confidence.

Lady Lavinia and Lady Mary enjoyed the evening also as Lord Dearham was politely attentive to them, too, and insisted they both danced one dance with him. Susan was delighted her début was such a success.

It was not until the end of the evening came, she realised that it had not been totally successful as she had not acquired an admirer. In fact the only chance she'd had was squashed by his lordship. They had just finished a dance when Susan had spied Monsieur Montgolfier.

'Why there's Jean-Paul!' she exclaimed.

She was surprised when his lordship had taken her elbow and pushed her in the opposite direction.

'It is best for you to avoid him.'

'But why? I thought he was your friend, my lord.'

'He is. He's a fine balloonist.'

Puzzled, Susan persisted.

'I find Jean-Paul most amusing. We seemed to deal well together. He tells me he is not married, and as I'm looking for a husband why shouldn't I try to win his affections?'

'I advise you to look elsewhere.'

Susan looked up at the earl enquiringly.

'Surely you trust him?'

'Not where pretty girls are concerned.'

Susan pouted prettily.

'My choice of a marriage partner is going to be restricted enough without you turning down all the possibilities.'

'I certainly would never want to stand in the way of your finding happiness, Miss Woodford. Believe me I'm as anxious as you are to see you happily settled, but as you are a most desirable young lady you can afford to take your time and choose with care. Your attraction will endure, so you must be patient, ma'am, and when the right man comes along for you I will be the first to encourage him.'

A flush of pleasure tinted Susan's face. He could say the nicest things. She cast a look into the card room where Jean-Paul was now surrounded by a cluster of women. His lordship was right. Jean-Paul was a womaniser.

Indeed, although his lordship was a reckless flyer, she had discovered he was not irresponsible. In truth the more time she spent with him the more she admired him. She prayed that night that she might meet a gentleman with as much integrity as Lord Dearham to marry.

* * *

The following morning a bouquet of roses was delivered from the Dearham Hall hot-houses for the ladies. Susan had hoped Lord Dearham might call, but neither he, nor any gentlemen did.

As both Mama and Lady Mary were fatigued after their night out they stayed in their rooms. Susan felt strangely restless, for she kept thinking about Lord Dearham, and by the afternoon decided that if she didn't go out she'd scream. She took Betty with her as a companion.

Betty, with her broad London accent and simple servant's clothes, was not really suitable as a young lady's companion, but Susan knew Betty would like a break from her work and enjoy an outing. The air was full of the scents of autumn, and a brisk walk in it would do them both good.

As they set out Susan inhaled the fresh air appreciatively. After only a few weeks in Bath she already knew her way around the streets and felt quite at home there. She never would have thought a short time ago the misery of her Papa's death and debts would have brought other than ruin to herself and Mama. Not that she didn't remember her Papa with a certain amount of affection.

She had loved him dearly as a child and it was only when she grew older that she began to see that he was a gambler, who was giving her poor mama constant humiliations and worry from tradesmen as he steadily gambled away her fortune.

Yet dear Mama had insisted on giving Susan a good education, and had denied herself so that her child might be brought up properly. Susan was sent to a good Ladies Seminary where not only reading, writing and arithmetic were taught, but French, deportment and dancing as well, all essential accomplishments for a young lady.

Susan was well aware that without her mother's sacrifice she would not have known how to behave in Society last night, and be able to perform the dances which she so enjoyed with Lord Dearham. But it was Lord Dearham and Lady Mary she was indebted to for being able to reside in the comfortable, convenient little house in Milsom Street. And Susan was delighted to see that her mother's reinstatement in Society had recovered her spirits.

Was it surprising that Lord Dearham kept cropping up in her mind when she owed him so much? Yet she still felt a little resentful to have to be a dependant of his. She would much prefer to find a husband who could support her. She really would have to try to find one.

A rosiness flamed her cheeks when she suddenly thought that if she did get married she would only be changing one man's support for another! Perhaps she should not be worrying about getting a husband. Even Lord Dearham had told her she need be in no hurry. She could be content to be protected and supported as she was at the moment.

Betty was trotting beside her chatting merrily when approaching them came a fashionably-attired couple, the lady wearing an outsized and highly decorative hat. Susan was embarrassed as she heard Betty exclaim.

'Lawks! The lady's like a porter's wife wiv a fruit basket on 'er 'ead.'

'Hush!' Susan hissed hoping her maid's remark had not been heard, and was relieved to be greeted by the couple as they passed by.

'Betty, you really must refrain from saying the first thing that comes into your head,' she scolded when they were alone again.

'I can't 'elp it miss. It just comes out.'

'Well, don't let it. I expect you to

make the effort to behave like gentlefolk when you are with them. They might think as you do, but they avoid making loud comments.'

'Yes, miss.'

Susan hid a smile. She knew she would never cure her, but she was fond of Betty.

But after twenty minutes Betty cried, 'Crimminy, 'ow much farther are we going, miss? My feet don't half ache. I wants me dinner, and Annie's said she's going to make a meat pudding.'

Susan could have walked farther but she said, 'Very well, Betty. We'll turn back now.'

Back down the busy street they went, passing the fragrant bakery shop, glancing in the hat maker's window, and seeing the tailors' and the cabinet-makers' signs. They were passing a man grinding scissors when Betty gave a cry.

'Oooh! Blow me if t'aint that 'andsome balloon flyer! Look over there, miss!'

Betty's squawks and pointing finger made Susan's blood race. Indeed there was Lord Dearham strolling along the opposite promenade, with a very beautiful young lady on his arm! Jealousy stabbed Susan. After dancing with him last night, to see him escorting another lady — a very fine lady, too — wounded her. And yet her common-sense told her she had no right to feel that way.

Before she could stop her, Betty was waving furiously, attracting the couple's attention.

'Betty, you shouldn't wave like that.'

'Why ever not, miss? 'E's seen us and he's grinning, and look 'e's coming over 'ere.'

It was true. Before Susan could escape, Lord Dearham and his lady were crossing the road towards her. Although neatly dressed, Susan had not yet completed her new wardrobe and she was immediately conscious of her inferior position and mortified that Betty had called them over. Of course

Lord Dearham could have acknowledged her and passed her by, but he seemed quite keen to speak to her.

'Good day to you, Miss Woodford,' he said heartily and bowed, although the lady with him gave her the slightest nod to her curtsey after the introductions.

'We . . . we would like to thank you for the flowers,' Susan said, her cheeks becoming annoyingly rosier.

'The pleasure is mine, Miss Woodford.'

He turned to his lady companion.

'We attended the Assembly Rooms last night, Arabella.'

'That is most unlike you, Tom!' the lady retorted putting her pert nose in the air. 'I thought you detested mixing with the hoi-poloi.'

Lord Dearham smiled.

'It was Miss Woodford's come out, and I enjoyed the evening very much.'

'So did Miss Susan,' Betty chipped in. 'She said you was the best dancer she'd ever hope to meet, and she said you was the most 'andsomest gentle'um there and — '

'That's enough, Betty.'

The lady's tinkling laugh, making it clear she thought it amusing the maid had blurted out how infatuated Susan was with his lordship. And her look suggested that she considered Miss Woodford to have little more breeding than her maid. Susan had gone scarlet. Lost for words she grasped her maid's hand.

'Excuse me, we must go,' she muttered.

But his lordship bowed and his steady gaze made her look up into his face. She could see he was not laughing at her. There was a kind expression on his face, as though he understood her discomfit and wanted to show he did not share his lady's attitude. She was sure of it when he smiled and winked at her.

When they parted, Susan's feet seemingly floated over the pavement. She basked in the warmth with which Lord Dearham had supported her. She felt elated because she realised now she really liked him. He'd become a friend. But at the same time she knew he was like a distant star in the heavens, he would never consider her his friend. He was way above her rank.

* * *

The next day, as Susan was helping Lady Mary in the still-room, making a pot-pourri, crushing sweet-smelling spices to mix with dried rose petals, Lady Mary mentioned that Lord Dearham had returned to London to stay in his town house.

'I really don't know what has made him change his habits in the last few weeks,' she said. 'Tom was so keen about ballooning, he couldn't spend enough time at it. Now all of a sudden he's unsettled, and off to town every five minutes.'

Susan knew that unsettled feeling very well. She'd been quite unlike herself recently, aimless, and unable to interest herself in reading or playing the piano. She didn't feel hungry either, only a strange longing to see his lordship again.

'I expect his lordship has many friends,' she said.

'Oh, indeed he has. But I sometimes wonder why he's never married. He needs to you know. An earl must beget an heir.'

Aware that Lady Mary was looking at her keenly, Susan said regretfully, 'Oh, I understand gentlemen of his standing trifle with many women.'

Lady Mary tutted.

'I think it is more likely women trifle with him! Just because he seems to have every advantage it does not mean he has been smitten by any of his lady friends. Although I think he may have found someone now.'

Arabella came into Susan's mind and she shuddered. Round-eyed with consternation Susan turned to Lady Mary. 'Who's the lady?'

Lady Mary, warming a dried orange in her hands to prepare it for a pomander, gave her a teasing smile and said, 'I think you will know quite soon.'

'I hope he'll choose with care,' Susan commented for, she couldn't bear to think of Lord Dearham unhappily married.

'That you need not fear. He's no fool.'

No, Susan thought sadly, but for all his intelligence I hope he does not make the mistake of marrying Arabella, because she would not make him happy.

In her bedchamber two days later Betty was helping Susan unpack the packages which had been delivered from the dressmaker's.

'Lawks!' Betty squeaked as each garment was revealed. 'Ain't it loverly?'

Soft underclothes and fashionable day gowns, bonnets, gloves and shoes lay displayed around the room. Susan was thrilled. She was now well dressed.

As she twisted this way and that in front of her cheval glass she admired the narrow-striped red and white gown she was wearing. Then she stopped to rub her fingers over her new soft wool cloak.

'Never in my life have I owned so many clothes. Now I can appear in Society like a lady.'

'You always was a lady, miss.'

'Thank you, Betty, and you look nice in your new clothes, too.'

Betty's ample figure looked even larger in the freshly-made and ironed cotton dress Susan had thoughtfully had made for her. The maid grinned from ear to ear as she smoothed down her new crisp apron and patted her cap.

'Good,' Susan said. 'So now we are ready to go up in the balloon tomorrow.'

Betty's face expressed alarm. Her fingers fidgeted with the corner of her apron.

'I can't say as I fancy going up into the sky, miss.'

'But you must come with me. A lady can't go on an excursion by herself.'

'T'ain't natural to fly.'

'Of course it is! Birds fly, so why shouldn't people?'

Betty began to fold the new underclothes and put them in the drawers.

‘I’m a lot ’eavier than a bird, miss, and I don’t ’ave wings neither.’

Susan could see the maid was unwilling to fly but tried to persuade her by saying, ‘Monsieur Montgolfier is an experienced aviator. He sent me a message this morning saying the weather is now suitable for going up in the balloon. Why, look out of the window you can see how mild and sunny it is. And think of the thrill of it. Many servants would love to have your opportunity to fly!’

‘They’re welcome to it.’

Susan became cross.

‘Betty, I don’t want to hear any more of your nonsense. I am going up in the balloon and so are you.’

Silence reigned as Betty finished putting the last of the new clothes away and slammed the last drawer shut.

She then stood up and said, ‘Yes, miss,’ before giving a bob and clattering out of the bedchamber.

Ashamed to have lost her temper with good-hearted Betty, Susan slumped on her bed and cupped her chin in her hands. Coercing a servant into doing what she did not want to do was not kind. The trouble was she had to have a female companion. She walked to the window and looked out. Indeed the weather was unusually clement for the time of the year. And they were only going up and down in the balloon. But she had to admit she felt most uneasy about it, too. If only Lord Dearham was going to be there she would feel entirely different about it — far less apprehensive.

But Lord Dearham had mentioned that Jean-Paul was an excellent balloonist. So she had nothing to fear. Anyway, she told herself, the flight would be over in less time than it would take to climb up to the top of St Paul's Cathedral dome and look out over the City of London.

6

Unfortunately for Susan the weather was still mild and sunny the following morning when the coach came to take her to Dearham Hall for the balloon flight, so she had no excuse for not going.

Lady Lavinia kissed her daughter goodbye and said she hoped Susan would enjoy the experience. Susan assured her mama that she was determined to. On the road Susan attempted to chase away Betty's sullens.

'I feel quite excited at the prospect of being up in the sunny sky today,' she said.

'I can't say I feel excited,' Betty snorted. 'Scared's more like it.'

'Oh, do stop nibbling your nails, Betty. There's nothing to be frightened of. It'll be over in a few minutes.'

But seeing the wind tossing the

remaining leaves on the bushes and trees, Susan felt as doubtful as her maid. She wrapped her cloak around her and hoped her new hat would not blow away when the balloon actually went up.

At Dearham Hall, Monsieur Montgolfier greeted Susan with profuse smiles as well as a flourishing bow.

'Am I the first lady to have a ride in a balloon, Jean-Paul?' she asked excitedly.

'Ah, non, mademoiselle! But I think you are the most beautiful,' he replied.

Susan did not feel flattered by his remark as she was well aware he was a flirt. When they entered the paddock, Susan's stomach lurched when she saw the massive red and orange striped balloon floating away above her in the sky. Filled with gas, it bobbed and tugged on its moorings as if anxious to be off.

Many helpers were there, but some men, Susan thought, seemed to look a little morose, unsure what they were supposed to be doing, and a few were fooling about. Perhaps they were just waiting for the passengers, she told herself.

On closer inspection, the wicker basket under the balloon appeared more puny than she'd remembered it, and her heartbeats quickened. But having made the French aviation scientist go to so much trouble to take her up in the sky she felt she couldn't refuse to go up now. She forced herself to smile and tried to show her appreciation by saying how much they were looking forward to their little adventure.

Betty mumbled something under her frilled cap as she hung her head. Susan knew Jean-Paul was knowledgeable about ballooning, but she wished with all her heart that Lord Dearham were present. The men seemed to miss his leadership and everyone seemed to miss his confident smile and good-humour.

'Jean-Paul,' she whispered to the Frenchman, 'are you sure it is wise for us to go up today? It has become a little more blowy, and look over there at those slate-coloured clouds in the sky.'

'But we have got everything all ready, mademoiselle.' Jean-Paul sounded peeved. 'We will only go up a little way and it will give you a marvellous view.'

Susan felt troubled. As they walked by some strange-looking apparatus, she felt her heart beating so loudly she wondered he did not comment on it.

'Ugh! It stinks,' Betty complained.

Jean-Paul raised an eyebrow and explained.

'Acid is poured over hot iron filings to make the gas that is held in those two water-bound casks. It is then fed into the balloon's envelope via those silken hoses.'

Susan was mystified but when she arrived at the balloon she got some comfort from noting that the netting covering the balloon was firmly secured to guy ropes and strong poles held it anchored.

'You see I have a box for you to step on and help you get into the gondola,' Jean-Paul said.

Betty's face was a picture of misery,

so Susan decided she must get in first to give her maid encouragement. But she hesitated before she did so, torn between deciding that she didn't want to, and thinking she could not refuse to at this late stage. It took all her courage to accept Jean-Paul's offered hand and step up on a box so that she could clamber into the basket. Once inside she looked out with quaking knees for Betty, and her heart stopped when she saw her maid haring off across the paddock towards the stables!

* * *

Lord Dearham had not enjoyed his days in London. Much as he tried to amuse himself with friends, nothing would interest him or remove Miss Woodford from his mind. He took Arabella to routs, concerts and to Ranelagh Gardens, and found them all dull. Her high-pitched voice and silly observations began to get on his nerves, while Miss Woodford's pleasant voice and pretty dimpled smile seemed to haunt him. He tried everything from gaming, to buying a new horse, but nothing seemed to relieve his agitation.

Waking up one morning and seeing the sun out and a playful wind blowing made him think it was the excitement of flying he was missing. He ordered his valet, Simpson, to pack his bags, and make ready to leave for Dearham Hall that afternoon.

The day being exceedingly fine, he decided to ride home and let his luggage be brought by wagon under the care of Simpson. He would spend the night with his grandparents in Melksham before riding on in the morning.

A fresh start from there in the morning got him to Dearham Hall by the afternoon, and his joy to be home was only marred by the fact that there seemed to be no grooms around the stables to care for his horse.

After taking the animal into a stall himself and removing the saddle and bridle, he began to give the animal a rub down when he heard a whimper.

Listening for a moment he decided it sounded like someone crying, so he began to search the stables. When he found a maid in the corner of a stall huddled in her cloak and sobbing her heart out, he frowned.

'What's the matter?'

When she sobbed all the louder, he crouched down beside her and asked soothingly, 'You are Miss Woodford's maid, Betty, are you not. Is she here at the Hall?'

Betty sobbed.

'Yes.'

'Well,' his lordship said, 'I daresay I might be able to help you if you'll tell me what's upsetting you.'

Red, wet eyes looked up at him.

'You're the flyer, ain't you, sir?'

'I am.'

Betty began to wipe her nose on her sleeve until his lordship's white handkerchief appeared which she took with a mumbled thank you. After blowing her nose and wiping her eyes,

Betty said, ‘Miss Woodford is cross with me.’

‘She’s frequently cross with me,’ his lordship said dryly. ‘What have you done to annoy her?’

‘I ain’t done nothing, sir. She’s not pleased just ’cos I was scared and wouldn’t fly with ’er.’

The awful possibility dawned on his lordship. Surely that accursed Frenchman, Jean-Paul, hadn’t decided to take Miss Woodford up in the balloon today? It was far too windy. But it would explain why there were no grooms around.

That French balloonist didn’t understand the variable English weather. His lordship had been reading the cloud formation riding home and he knew stormy weather was in the air.

He patted Betty’s shoulder and said, ‘No, you’ve done nothing wrong, Betty. You are a sensible girl not wanting to fly today.’

He rose to his feet.

‘And if Miss Woodford is thinking of

flying, I'll soon put a stop to it.'

Marching out of the stables, he strode towards the paddock, but when he saw the balloon bouncing around in the air he cursed and began to run.

* * *

Alarm had pierced Susan. When she was left in the balloon's basket and her maid had scampered off. She wanted to get out.

'Monsieur Montgolfier!'

A cry from one of the men sent Jean-Paul scurrying off to see what he wanted, leaving Susan to get out of the basket without his assistance.

Alarm turned to panic as Susan realised it was impossible for her, in her long skirts, to climb over the rim of the basket alone. The situation soon became a nightmare as she realised the men were trying to hold the dancing balloon against the pull of the wind. She heard Jean-Paul screaming a volley of instructions in French, forgetting the men would not understand a word of what he was trying to tell them.

A male chorus of irate roars sounded as another sharp blast of wind sent the balloon jerking to free itself from its moorings. Susan was sent tumbling as the gondola lurched and as she pulled herself up she realised to her horror that the balloon was trying to fly away, with her inside alone!

'Please God, save me,' she cried.

With tears in her eyes she blinked. A man was racing toward the balloon as fast as his long legs would take him. Her prayer had been answered. It was Lord Dearham coming to her rescue!

But as he came with arms outstretched to grab the basket there was an ominous hiss of gas. Men hollered as a mighty gust of wind sent the basket dragging across the grass.

Then all was calm. Susan breathed with relief. His lordship must have caught hold of one of the ropes and was holding it still. But, no, that was impossible! Glancing anxiously over the edge of the basket she saw open-mouthed men watching her. And they were beginning to look smaller and smaller, as she was being moved away from them.

She was airborne!

Too fearful to scream, she did not notice at first two lace-ruffled shirt cuffs and two large hands gripping the rim of the basket, until a man's boot was flung over the top.

'Help me up, dammit!'

Susan's body froze as she darted to grasp his muscular leg with one hand, and a handful of his coat with the other. Sobbing lest he might fall to his death, she strained to tug the struggling man aboard. He grunted with the effort, but managed to hoist himself up at last and fell into the gondola, knocking Susan over with him.

Panting, they regarded each other until Susan managed to gasp, 'I thought you were in London, my lord.'

'I was,' he said catching his breath, 'but every time I go . . . I find . . . I have to come back to bail you out of trouble.'

A relieved Susan relaxed a little seeing his wry grin until she noticed he was studying her revealed ankle. She quickly straightened her skirts and stood up noticing the balloon was sailing over a tree. If he had not been with her, she would be terrified.

'Thank you for rescuing me, my lord.'

'I would say you were far from being rescued!'

The basket swayed and seemed to be sailing higher into the sky.

'Well, you are going to get us down, I hope,' she said with a nervous giggle.

'So do I!' he said springing to his feet and looking out.

Grasping a sack of sand which was on the floor of the basket he heaved it over the side.

'What are you doing?'

'I'm trying to prevent us from crash landing on the roof of the Hall, Miss Woodford. If we lighten the load, the balloon will rise.'

And Susan looked to see that they

were indeed floating over Dearham Hall, skimming the roof by inches. Smooth air currents soon swept them away and Susan felt her stomach jump as her body was thrust higher and higher as the balloon veered westward away from Dearham Hall.

'Where are we going?'

A grunt was his only reply. Yet when she looked down at the miniature world below her feet, she was fascinated to stare at the panorama of woods, fields and hills, tiny white specks that she knew to be sheep grazing, and toy-sized farms. She recognised a stretch of the river looking like a silver ribbon as it sparkled in the sun.

'The view's incredible!' she exclaimed.

He moved to her side.

'Yes, indeed it is,' he agreed and she caught the excitement in his voice.

If he was not afraid neither need she be. Twisting her head she looked up at his sparkling eyes and for a moment or two they shared the exhilaration of flying. A sudden gust of wind buffeted the balloon and if it were not for his lordship's hand coming around her shoulder to steady her she might have toppled over.

The weather was changing. The sun had disappeared. They flew through the misty whiteness of a cloud, and Susan was thankful for her warm cloak Jean-Paul had advised her to bring.

'Shall we go back now?' she shivered.

He flicked back his tousled hair revealing his flinty eyes.

'You amaze me,' he shouted over the wind. 'I don't understand how an intelligent woman can expect me to stop this thing and turn it around as though it were a pony cart!'

Conscious she deserved the rebuke, she kept her voice serene as she asked, 'Where will we land?'

'That is the question I am asking myself. And if you dislike the cold, you should have thought of the consequences before you accepted Jean-Paul's offer to take you flying.'

Susan opened her mouth to protest that she understood she was merely going up and down not making a tour of the countryside, but as she was so glad she had his lordship with her, and not Jean-Paul, she did not reply. Seeing he'd quelled her he grimaced.

'It's not your fault,' he blurted out. 'Jean-Paul should never have let you near the balloon in this variable weather. And I am to blame, too. I should never have given him permission.'

Susan could not hear the rest of his words because of the noise of the thrumming of the guy ropes. But she found it comforting to know he didn't put all the blame on her.

She had to accept that they were now in a fix, and that although she felt safe with his lordship he was obviously having difficulty grounding the craft, and she feared she might have to endure far more discomfort before they landed.

She heard him say, 'You have courage, I'll say that for you, Miss Woodford. Any other female would be hysterical by now.'

For a moment, they turned to face one another. Her pretty face looked pinched with cold, yet no word of complaint had she made. He admired her mettle and his mouth twitched into a smile. She smiled back at him. Little did he know how frightened she was!

'I don't think hysterics would help matters,' she said calmly.

He laughed.

'You're right.'

His attention was taken by trying to find a break in the low clouds. He leaned so far out of the basket Susan clutched him.

After a while he called out, 'Ah, I think I can detect a mass of buildings below us. I believe we are over Bristol.'

Susan peered down and saw the craft was skimming over houses, parks, churches and some people were staring up at them.

'That's Queen's Square,' he shouted

excitedly. 'We are heading towards Durham Downs, a safe landing place.'

He pulled a handle to open the valve, letting some gas escape to lower the balloon.

'It won't be long now.'

His voice trailed away as another powerful gust of wind swept the balloon off course.

'Damn this wind!'

Dense cloud had built up around them again. For a tense few minutes Susan heard him saying something to himself about the possibility of landing on Crockle Hill. But when the clouds dispersed they saw water and ship's rigging over the docks.

The thought of them drifting helplessly towards the sea made her gasp in terror. She felt his warm hand grasp hers and his thumb stroke the back of her hand in a comforting manner.

'Wales, here we come!' he cried.

Feeling reassured she quipped, 'I've always wanted to visit Wales. I've heard it's most picturesque.'

He chuckled. Minute by minute they were sailing away from England into wild Wales, and a misty drizzle shrouded them.

'Look, we are over Newcome Sands. I can see we are coming to moorland,' he shouted with glee. 'We can go down. Now, my love you are going to have to be very brave as the landing will jar us.'

My love! He had called her, my love, the term of endearment he used for his Aunt Mary. Susan felt cold, wet and frightened, but her heart glowed with the warmth of his words. Their descent seemed rapid, more like a fall towards the ground, and his lordship gathered her to his body in one arm while releasing the last of the gas with the other. Rushing wind sounded in her ears.

'We're almost down. Hold tight on to me,' he yelled.

With a skeleton-rattling bump the basket struck the earth, rose again and crashed down once more. Tearing over the hummocks of grass, rocks jagged the basket as the collapsing envelope was towed by the wind. Cradled in his arms, Susan heard the basket splitting and felt herself being dragged along the ground, until she felt a sharp pain.

She must have fainted because the next thing she knew she was lying on grass, soaked, as it was raining. She looked up to see herself surrounded by some small black cattle who were mooing gently at her.

7

As the startled cattle moved back, Susan couldn't see his lordship. All she could see around her was more of the rain-swept moor where she'd fallen. Trying to stand, she felt a stab of pain in her foot and fell back on the rain-sodden grass with a groan.

Gritting her teeth she told herself to endure the pain. She had to find Lord Dearham. She managed to stand and, removing the damp strands of hair that clung to her face obliterating her vision, looked around. What she saw made her want to weep. There was nothing but endless moor, and a few curious cattle who were nosing the remains of the machine which was lying about.

Then her heart leaped. She heard him calling. His lordship had not been killed! Rising out of a clump of shrubs a familiar tall figure came towards her.

But what a sight he looked!

His matted hair hung down like a wet mop; his fine riding coat was ripped and his cravat looked like a limp and dirty rag. But then, how did she appear to him? Her hair was undone, her new cloak and hat missing. And as for the state of her gown, why it was soiled and torn, too! His smile when he saw her lifted her spirits, and she hobbled to meet him.

'I see you are hurt,' he said, his face grave, and coming up to her he put his arms around her.

How good it felt to have him with her, to have his strong body supporting her.

'Please don't concern yourself about me, my lord,' she said. 'I've only jarred my ankle. Were you hurt?'

She thought of how he'd protected her during the landing and must be sore. He shrugged.

'Just a few scrapes. I'll recover,' he said cheerfully.

That she believed, but remarked sadly, 'I regret your balloon is — '

'Destroyed? I know. But that's a risk I take every time I fly. Never mind, we had a good flight, didn't we?'

'Indeed we did, my lord. It was a wonderful experience.'

With rivulets of rain running down their faces their eyes met and they grinned at each other, and then broke into laughter.

'I think you should call me Tom now. And if you will allow it, I shall call you Susan.'

He was right. They were in the wilds of Wales, far from Society. Susan smiled as she nodded. Then her dimples vanished.

'What shall we do now?'

His face became thoughtful as he put his hand on his forehead and his eyes scanned the horizon.

'That's the problem. I don't know where we are. I can't see anything. I think we should follow the animal tracks over there until we find some shelter.'

The thought of walking on her sore foot didn't appeal to Susan, but she had no choice. She found as they set off that with Tom's arm around her it was a help.

The moor seemed to go on for ever, and the wind and rain determined to make their search for shelter more laborious.

Their chirpy remarks died out as they both felt the strain of plodding along the hoof tracks for what seemed like miles. Wincing at the stab of pain she felt every time she put her left foot down was not pleasant, but having Tom so close was a tremendous comfort.

'The light is fading,' she gasped eventually. 'Leave me here and go on. I'm slowing you down.'

'Bear up a little longer, Susan. I'm sure we'll find somewhere soon,' he replied.

Just when she thought she really could go on no longer, he cried, 'I'm sure I see a light ahead. Maybe a farmhouse.'

Susan also saw a glimmer of light ahead but in her exhausted state it seemed almost too far, but the hope of finding refuge and Tom's encouragement spurred her on.

Barking dogs rushed towards them. Susan instinctively pressed herself nearer Tom as the small, pricked-eared hounds bounded around them yapping noisily.

'Don't be frightened, Susan. I've seen these Welsh corgi dogs before, at the market. They are trained to snap near the cattle's legs to herd them, but they don't bite.'

After a while, the dogs quietened down and wagged their stubby tails, forming an escort for the bedraggled pair as they walked towards the buildings. A man holding a lantern came out of his cottage door. On seeing them he called out something. Tom waved and hollered back.

'What did he say?' Susan asked.

'We won't understand him I'm afraid. He speaks Welsh. We'll have to try to make him think our carriage has broken down and we got lost on the moor. The people here might burn us as witches if we explain that we flew in from the heavens!'

Tom's ready smile helped as he greeted the farmer, and a rotund woman appeared and ushered Susan into the cottage, seating her by the smokey turf fire in the range.

The motherly woman rushed to get a towel and dry clothes, chatting away in a torrent of Welsh, making Susan strip off her wet garments as if she were a child, ignoring the men in the background.

Clothed in a voluminous shift, her shoulders covered by a cosy Welsh shawl and her feet in sheep's wool slippers, Susan felt warm, and sleepy. While the woman dried and combed her hair, she looked to see that Tom had changed, too, and was wearing some patched, workmen's clothes.

'The Welsh are not a tall race,' he grinned, pulling at his short sleeves and breeches legs.

The hospitable Welsh woman bustled

to fill bowls of hot stew from the cooking pot which hung over the fire, and making Tom sit by Susan on a settle, she gave them the bowls, cut them hunks of bread, and urged them to eat. The food tasted delicious but Susan was too tired to eat more than a few mouthfuls.

She became aware of Tom gently taking the bowl from her hands, then of him picking her up and carrying her to an adjoining room where she was placed on a straw-mattressed bed. In the blessed warmth she soon fell asleep.

⋆ ⋆ ⋆

Sometime in the early morning a cock crowed and Susan stirred. For a moment, she wondered where on earth she was. Although warm and comfortable, she knew she wasn't in her own bed. Of course, she was in Wales after the disastrous balloon flight!

She felt someone on the bed beside her. She raised herself on her elbow and looked over at the sleeping body, which in the daybreak light she could just see. She was not at first sure who it was. But one thing she was sure of. It was a long body because feet were sticking out of the end of the bed.

There was only one tall person in the Welsh cottage, the Earl of Dearham!

Shocked, she sat upright, drawing the cover partially off his sleeping body. Then she saw the red weals over his neck, and arms, and as his nightshirt was open she could see the top of his bruised shoulders, injuries she'd been spared because he'd protected her during the crash landing. Torn between wanting to kick him out of her bed, and feeling a pang of compassion that he'd suffered so much, she sat immobile until she heard him murmur.

'Egad, you've taken all the bed-clothes!'

He yanked them back and covered his shoulders.

'Snuggle down and go to sleep. We've a long journey back to England in the morning and we need to rest,' he told her.

Susan lay back on the pillow breathing shakily. He'd got into bed with her and destroyed her reputation! But, as she thought about it, she realised that her reputation was already destroyed when she flew off in the balloon with him, and did not return immediately. It was as bad as eloping in the eyes of Society.

She turned her head and could just see his handsome face as he slept. He looked like an innocent babe. She felt the urge to touch him, and smoothed back the long fringe from his closed eyes, as she had so often seen him do. Then before she'd thought whether she should or not she bent over and kissed him!

She now knew how her mother had felt when she fell in love. Reasoning that as a single girl with no means she should marry a respectable man who would support her took no account of her feelings. Despite her resolve, she'd fallen for this man. And she knew she would always love Tom, for ever, no matter what he did. Even if he married Arabella!

But she now also realised that Tom was not at all like her father. He was not the same type of man. Tom had shown himself to be a brave, caring and responsible man. She felt certain Lord Dearham would not do anything dishonourable, and felt safe lying beside him. The kindly Welsh couple had probably given their only bed to their visitors. The good Welsh couple probably thought they were married anyway.

Satisfied she was in no danger, sleep overtook her before she had time to worry about her future.

A thundering sound woke Susan up. It came from outside the cottage.

Tom had gone! When her feet touched the ground, she felt her ankle was still sore, but she got to the window and looked out. The little cattle were being herded by some men on horseback and were being helped by the dogs.

Feeling she should be up, too, Susan looked back into the room and saw her clothes, all dry and laid out for her to wear. How hospitable the Welsh were she thought as she dressed herself, noticing that some of the worst tears in her garments had been sewn together.

Leaving the bedroom she opened the door and found herself looking into the cottage kitchen. The farmer's wife was feeding a baby, while an older infant was playing with wooden toys on the floor. There was no sign of Tom. Carrying her baby the woman smiled and pointed to the table where platters were laid.

Susan's nose was twitching with the delicious smell of bacon and although she wanted to go out and search for Tom, she sat down at the table as she was bid. Then she offered to hold the dear little baby while a cooked breakfast was prepared for her.

The toddler came up to show Susan his toys and for a short time she enjoyed playing with the two Welsh children.

Having finished her tasty breakfast, and not knowing how to thank the good woman, Susan smiled and kissed her, sending the motherly woman into wreaths of smiles and much more unintelligible Welsh!

Going outside, she was thankful for the shawl she'd been urged to wear. It was chilly, but a fine day. How green and glistening the moorland was now, quite beautiful. Then she spied some swarthy drovers, talking and laughing with Lord Dearham.

Seeing her, Tom smiled and waved before leaving the men and striding over to her. He was wearing his own clothes again, but like hers, they looked shabby.

When he came close she suddenly felt coy, remembering he'd shared her bed, and felt herself colour. But he didn't tease her, instead he looked at her sympathetically.

'Good morning, Susan. How's your foot?'

'It has greatly recovered,' she answered. Then without thinking she was not supposed to have seen them, she asked, 'And how are your injuries?'

Like a true gentleman he didn't hint how she knew about his injuries and he answered easily.

'Still uncomfortable, but a good night's sleep helped.'

So it seemed he would not embarrass her by mentioning where they'd spent the night. It would be their secret not to be mentioned. Susan appreciated his reticence. She knew that once they were back in Bath things would be different, but while they were together she could relax and enjoy his company.

'Can you ride?' he enquired.

'Years ago, before my father lost his money, I had a pony.'

'Good. We are fortunate that the drovers are here today to collect some cattle to take to market in Chepstow. We can go with them, and we'll be off as soon as they bring you a mount.'

The Welsh pony they found for Susan delighted her. At a drover's command, the little corgis scurried around the herd of cattle yapping to start them moving away from the farm. Tom thanked the farmer and his wife, slipping them some guineas, and then set off with Susan on the trek back to England.

8

As they rode side by side, Susan sensed a new closeness between them and wondered if Lord Dearham felt it also. In the past he'd called her rude, and she'd been so cross with him she'd thrown a book at him! But now she admired and loved him, and she hoped his opinion of her had altered for the better. Anyway she now felt she could talk to him more easily.

'Mama will be worried not knowing what has happened to us,' she said looking up at him.

'Aunt Mary will comfort her.'

'Yes, I suppose she will, only . . .'

It was hard to explain to a man that her mother would be worrying about her daughter's reputation. He gave her a smile.

'Aunt Mary was a great comfort to me when I was a small, motherless boy,' he said gently.

Susan found it difficult to imagine the tall, broad-shouldered man riding with her as a defenceless child, but now she knew he could feel vulnerable. There were times he didn't always feel as self-assured as he looked, and realising that made her feel another link had been forged between them, because although she might give him the impression she was a totally confident woman, inside she didn't always feel she was.

'I think Jean-Paul will have reassured the ladies that balloon flying is quite safe,' he added.

'How can you say that?'

'Well it is. It was the wind that caused our difficulties. The theory of flying has been known by scholars for years. Flying in a well-made balloon is as safe as taking a carriage drive.'

'Indeed? And where is your balloon now, m'lord?'

He laughed.

'You are quite right. I haven't an aerostatic machine any longer. But as it happens I'll have other things to occupy my mind.'

He gave her a wink.

Not knowing what he meant, and thinking that although his expensive balloon had been destroyed he was taking it very well, she said humbly, 'I'm truly sorry I was the cause.'

'Don't go blaming yourself again. It was fate. Although I can't wait to get my hands on Jean-Paul!'

She smiled, knowing he was funning because she did not think it was in his nature to be vindictive.

'You were quite right about that Frenchman,' she said. 'He is not to be trusted. I'm so glad I have you here on this adventure, and not him.'

He gave her a beautiful smile which sent her insides reeling.

'I was hoping you thought well of me.'

'Why, I owe you so much, my lord!'

'You owe me nothing, and I seem to remember I asked you to address me as Tom.'

'I can't when we get home.'

'Indeed you shall.'

Susan thought wryly that he didn't seem to appreciate the difficulty she would be in when they arrived back in Bath. He wouldn't be criticised for being alone with her, but being alone with him had left her compromised, and her quest to find a respectable husband was probably at risk. She would have to be content to be a spinster. She felt disappointed he did not seem to think of her dreary future. Yet being in love with him gave her a lovely feeling, too, and illogical though it was, she couldn't imagine anything but good could come of it.

A drover's call suddenly resounded across the majestic verdant Welsh valley as the black cattle streamed along the hill tracks. It was fascinating to watch the skill with which the drovers set about their difficult task of herding the plodding beasts mile after mile. The sun shone, making wondrous lights and dancing shadows, and the sky was a moving picture of great clouds. Truly Wales was a beautiful country as people said it was, and it made a memorable setting for the ride she was enjoying with the man she loved, the man, alas, who could never be hers.

Soon after midday, they stopped to rest and water the animals at a busy drovers' station. While the cattle and ponies rested in enclosed fields, Susan and Tom sat down with the drovers and ate a lunch of coarse barley bread, potatoes and herrings, washed down with cider. The drovers were cheerful company. Their English guests couldn't understand their tongue but they watched as the drovers chatted merrily as they ate, sharing jokes and even having a sing-song at the end of the meal.

Tom, who sat next to Susan, suddenly put his hand over hers and asked, 'Are you able to continue, my love?'

Bewildered by his endearment and that he continued to cover her hand she confessed, 'As I'm not used to riding,

I'm feeling a little saddle-sore, but I'll manage.'

'Good girl!' he exclaimed. 'You're a wonderful, spirited lady!'

The compliment crimsoned her cheeks. She looked at him and found he wanted to look deeply into her eyes, too. For one moment she wished they were not surrounded by people and he would take her in his arms. But he hadn't said that he loved her, only that he admired her spirit. He was just encouraging her to keep going. And yet, there was a tenderness in those soft brown eyes of his, as if he was trying to tell her something. As the call from the drovers made them go to collect their mounts she hoped she'd have the opportunity to find out.

As the slow-moving drove resumed, Susan began to feel less enamoured with the journey. As the miles passed she began to feel achy and tired, the pain in her ankle began to throb and her thighs chafed without a proper riding habit to protect her legs. But she was determined not to complain, and she knew Tom was also suffering from his lacerations and she noticed him wince and shift in his saddle once or twice.

It became markedly colder when the sun went in, and darker, too, as low rain clouds hovered over them. Susan saw a woodland ahead and didn't like the idea of having to enter the gloomy place, but the track led through it and the drovers were rounding the cattle up, forming them into a column, rubbing flanks as they walked along the narrow tree-lined road.

Susan followed Tom helping to prevent the cattle straying into the wood. It was dismal under the trees. The steady thundering of many hooves made her feel that step by step they were getting through the wood, and she would be glad when they had. Even her pony seemed restless. Then suddenly a gun fired and then another.

Shouts, cries and frightened animal noises produced sudden confusion.

Susan watched in dismay as the cattle's eyes rolled as they stopped walking and began to fidget. Some reared up. The corgis began to race around, barking excitedly, as the orderly procession through the wood broke into chaos.

'What's happened?' Susan cried over the drovers' cries.

Tom stood in his stirrups as he looked ahead. He muttered a curse.

'I fear it may be brigands trying to steal some of the poor Welsh farmers' cattle. I've heard they plan these raids in difficult places and lie in wait for the herd to appear.'

As he spoke, Susan's eyes widened. Shadowy horses with riders were emerging from the interior of the wood. Then she saw ahead that as the drovers were trying to urge the cattle onwards, the brigands were attempting to hive off some of the animals by cracking whips around them and forcing them into the woods.

Susan cried out in anger as she saw the havoc, and the lashes being cruelly laid over the tired beasts, and when a corgi yelped and dragged its injured body into the undergrowth near them, Tom gripped her arm, staying her attempt to dismount and go to its aid. Tom cursed as he assessed the disarray, and when a young drover was deliberately knocked off his pony and the other drovers went to help him up lest he was trampled underfoot, he hissed to Susan, 'Stay here.'

Slipping from his horse, Tom slipped between the two cows to where he'd spied the brigand chief who sat solid on his mount waving his gun and shouting orders to his men. Tom stealthily closed in behind the villain, then leaped on to his back, dragging him off his horse on to the ground.

The brigands soon became aware that their chief had been attacked and abandoned the raid. Preying on droves was their livelihood, but occasionally the drovers brought with them extra men to protect the herds from thieves. Seeing their leader felled made them nervous. Would they be caught and hanged?

As the brigands moved to assist their chief they let the cattle go, and the drovers, helped by their corgis, quickly rounded up the beasts and sent them lumbering safely out of the wood. Susan hesitated, not knowing whether to go with the drovers or remain with Tom's pony.

'Tom!' she cried anxiously, not noticing a man behind her until a large dirty hand clamped over her mouth.

She stiffened, her cries muffled as she felt herself being dragged off her pony and her arms pinned behind her back. Several leering, unshaven faces appeared before her terrified eyes. But what she saw farther ahead made her wrench her head free.

'Stop it!' she screeched seeing the scoundrels using their whips on Tom who was lying powerless on the ground.

The man holding her jerked her arms painfully.

'Don't worry about 'im. 'E ain't going

to last long. But we may 'ave a little use for you.'

Susan didn't hear their guffaws. She wasn't going to stand there and attempt nothing to save the man she loved. She was made of sterner stuff.

'You idiots!' she screamed. 'He's Lord Dearham. If you kill him you'll get no ransom for him, and the law will come and hunt you down.'

The half-English, half-Welsh babble that followed made her close her eyes and pray. It worked. The brigands ceased thrashing Tom. The brigand chief came swaggering up to her.

'How do we know you ain't lying?'

Had she not been accustomed to seeing and hearing coarse men in the London markets Susan may have felt frightened, but she held her ground.

'Take a look at his clothes and see that he has far too good a tailor to be a farmer.'

As the chief left her and stood astride Tom's prone and bleeding body she prayed his lordship was not already dead. Bending to examine Tom's clothing he snarled, 'These are gentleman's clothes all right, expensive stuff.'

He returned to Susan and pressed his dirty finger-nail under her defiant chin. It was agony to have to stare back at his hideous face but she did, just as she'd stood up to Mr Borman in the past.

'Now, who did you say this fellow is?'

Relief swept over her hearing him telling her Tom was still alive.

'He's the Earl of Dearham. Send word to Dearham Hall near Bath and they'll send you some gold for his safe return.'

The brigand rubbed his filthy hands together.

'And maybe you as 'is wife is worth summat?'

Susan didn't deny it, being thought of as Tom's wife might save her, too.

After conferring, the brigands mounted their horses. One hoisted Tom over his horse with him, while another roughly pulled her up in front of him so she could not escape. It was a long, wretched ride to their hideout. Susan, who was bounced up and down, cried out for mercy but received none. She wondered if poor Tom's battered body would survive the punishment. But before long her senses numbed, and her mind went blank as she lost consciousness.

Eventually they arrived at a ruined building where her aching body was pulled off the horse. She became aware of being carried and thrust into a cold cellar. Shivering and shaking Susan heard the men's footsteps retreat, and a solid door slam, leaving her in utter darkness. Terrified by a faint noise, wondering if it was a rat, she raised her battered body to peer around the dank cell, but all she saw, when she became accustomed to the dark, was a small, high window. Then she realised Tom was lying on the floor near her.

'Oh, Tom, they've killed you!' she cried crawling over to the still body.

'Not quite,' she heard him croak.

Sobs of relief overcame her at his

bravery. Tenderly she stroked his face and kissed him until she felt sticky blood where the horsewhip had cut him deeply. He had been seriously injured and would die if she didn't get him out of the freezing cellar. But how? She clamped her hands over her face. One thing was sure, despair would not release him from their prison. She had to do something.

Getting painfully to her feet she explored the small room using her hands on the rough-hewn stones, but there was nothing in the room. She came across steps which led up to the oak door. Climbing up and feeling all over the planks she found the rusty handle but the door was tightly closed.

Fatigue and desperation made her cry and fall against the door and to her amazement it gave way and creaked open a few inches. It wasn't locked! No doubt the old key had been lost, and the robbers thought their captives were too weakened to try to escape. But they hadn't reckoned on one spirited, young lady! Another shove and the door opened farther, enough for her to squeeze through. There was no sign of a guard outside, only more darkness.

'Tom, Tom, we can get out of here!' she said in a hushed voice as she kneeled by him.

His moan told her of his pain, but she shook him.

'Thomas Dearham,' she scolded, 'you must rouse yourself and get up. The door to our prison is open.'

'Egad, Susan, if you only knew how sliced up I am.'

'I do know, but you'll die if you stay here. And I can't lift you.'

'You are a demanding woman,' he grumbled as with low grunts he struggled to rise.

Tears ran down her face knowing the pain he must be suffering. Getting him up the steps in the darkness was a nightmare, but Susan insisted he did and, panting with the effort, they finally got there, and urged the door to give way enough to allow them through.

Their achievement seemed to give Tom new energy. He clamped her hand in his and led the way along a passage.

'Look ahead,' he whispered.

A starlit sky showed they were coming out of the darkness. A pale moon showed racing clouds, and roofless walled areas.

'This is an old border fort,' Tom said quietly. 'We must find the horses. But go cautiously. We don't want to disturb the brigands.'

The old castle grounds were like a maze. The sturdily-built hall that had once held a garrison of soldiers had crumbled with time, and everywhere jagged stones could trip them up. A yapping dog made them halt and cling to each other. Tom swore. Alert for the brigands to appear, they held their breath, but all they saw were two prick-eared corgis who came tearing up to them and began yapping at their heels.

'Shh!' Tom commanded the dogs and they stopped barking and sat down panting. 'They've been sent to find us,' he said as Susan bent down to pat the little fellows.

A neigh, horses whinnying and the pungent smell of manure told them the stables must be near. If Tom had been showing great bravery in bearing the pain inflicted on his whipped body so far, the ultimate test came for him as he selected a horse to ride. The easy life of the young earl had not prepared him for his agonising pain, his physical weakness, and the grit he needed to mount it. But when he saw Susan struggling to bridle a horse then gamely clamber on a pile of straw to get astride the big animal, they smiled wryly at each other as they sweated and suffered together, and he forced himself to get up behind her.

Once mounted, the corgis trotted ahead, leading the way. Without the dogs to guide them they would not have known which way to go, but the horse soon got the idea it had to follow the dogs. Afraid they would be heard and spotted, they made slow, cautious progress out of the stables and then over open countryside and into woodland. Sure-footed but much smaller in size than the horse, the little dogs led them along some tracks so narrow that the horse and riders found it difficult to get through.

Alarm stiffened them as the sound of horsemen made the corgis yap. Sickened to think that after all their effort to escape they would be captured again, Susan felt Tom's drooping body behind her and grasped his hands. The horse stopped and pawed the ground.

A sudden barking followed and more corgis appeared. Susan recognised some Welsh-speaking drovers who, with members of the Chepstow militia, surrounded them. Thank God, they were safe.

* * *

Early risers milling about the Golden Fleece Inn yard at Chepstow stood agape when a large party of riders and yapping heelers crowded in. And when they saw an unconscious and bloodied young man lifted gently off a horse and were told the injured gentleman was the Earl of Dearham who had been attacked by brigands, someone ran to tell the innkeeper who had the injured man borne upstairs to his best chamber. A doctor was sent for immediately.

When the hubbub died away, Susan was escorted inside the inn and helped up to a bedchamber where a kindly maidservant assisted her to undress and wash, found her a spare nightgown and then presented her with a warm drink before she was put into a bed which a copper warming pan had made blissfully comfortable. Susan lay back and fell into oblivion.

9

At Milsom Street, Lady Lavinia waited anxiously hour after hour to know if her daughter was safe. Jean-Paul's explanation about what had happened didn't reassure her one bit. But knowing Lord Dearham was with Susan made the situation seem far less of a calamity.

When at last news arrived by a galloping messenger to say they had been found, Susan's mama walked upstairs as fast as she could to tell Lady Mary, with tears of joy in her eyes.

Lady Mary, who had been equally worried about the destiny of the young couple said, 'That is indeed good news. Now do sit down, Lavinia, and calm yourself. May I see the message?'

Reading it to the end, which Lady Lavinia had failed to do, Mary frowned.

'I see Tom has been badly hurt. I must go to him at once.'

Lady Lavinia, who was dabbing her face with her handkerchief, exclaimed, 'Oh, dear! He's such a sweet boy.'

'He most certainly is, and honourable, too. You must realise, Lavinia, he has to marry Susan now. And I will make sure, when I see him, that he knows Society will expect him to do so.'

Lady Lavinia clasped her hands together smiling rapturously.

'Oh, Mary, I couldn't be happier hearing you say they should marry. I wish it dearly, too, but, I do wonder at times if Susan really likes Lord Dearham. I've seen them bicker a great deal, and she can be most stubborn, and may refuse him.'

'Well, I am convinced they are in love, but may not be aware of it yet.'

'I do so hope you are right, Mary.'

'And so do I. Now, I don't think you should travel with me, Lavinia, as the weather is turning wintry and you are not fully recovered from your illness. But while I'm gone you can start making secret plans for Susan's wedding. Now, if I may, I will borrow your maid, Betty, to accompany me. She can take some clothes for Susan. Annie can stay here with you and will see to your needs.'

The matter settled, the house was soon full of activity as Lady Mary prepared to set off for Chepstow. She sent a message to Lord Dearham's valet, telling him to take the mail coach to Chepstow that very afternoon. Patrick was instructed to hire a travelling coach for the morrow, and while Betty packed some things for Susan, Annie assisted Lady Mary.

When the coach arrived early the next morning, Lady Mary and Betty seated themselves inside with muffs to keep their hands warm and their booted feet resting on hot bricks. Patrick scrambled up to sit with the coachman, holding a blunderbuss on his lap because he'd heard there were brigands around Chepstow.

'I feel awful, ma'am,' Betty confessed to Lady Mary as the coach started on its way. 'I left Miss Susan to go up in the balloon by 'erself. Now she'll be in trouble being all alone with Lord Dearham. What are people going to say about her?'

'Nothing,' Lady Mary said severely, 'if you keep your mouth shut. I don't know exactly what happened to them when the balloon sailed away, and neither do you. Good servants don't spread scurrilous gossip about their mistress if they respect her, do they, Betty?'

'No, ma'am.'

Betty shuffled on her seat and bit her lip.

'Anyways, I like Miss Susan.'

'I know you do, and that is why you are pleased to know that she'll be getting married soon, although we will not mention it to anyone.'

'Yes, ma'am. I mean no,' Betty said, looking baffled.

* * *

Susan spent the next day in bed recovering from fatigue and her many bruises. She anxiously asked the maid who brought her some broth how Lord Dearham was faring.

'I only know he's very ill,' the maid replied, then seeing how white Susan had gone, added, 'but the doctor says he'll recover.'

Susan's request to see his lordship was approved by the doctor the following day. The doctor had done all he could to help Lord Dearham and thought as he was a strong, young man he should heal in time, and as his lordship kept asking to see the young lady, she was probably his best medicine he could have.

The maid found a dressing-gown for Susan to wear and she was shown into his lordship's sickroom, where his valet, Simpson, had done his best to improve his lordship's appearance.

Tom lay still and pale in bed propped up on many pillows. He opened his eyes when she approached and a ghost of a smile lit his sore face.

'Susan,' he breathed, trying to rise.

'Please don't exert yourself,' she said, taking the hand he offered her and holding it.

He had changed. His face no longer had the boyish, carefree appearance it had when she first met him. A scar ran down the side of his left eye. His gaunt look reminded her of a weathered soldier and made him look years older. His hair had been cut shorter, and he would no longer have to brush his long fringe away from his eyes.

'You look tired, Susan,' he said with difficulty, but as graciously as a lord. 'Are you being looked after?'

'Yes, thank you. I'm a little weary, but much recovered,' she answered, but she could see he was taut with pain.

It hurt her watching him, and she longed to do something to relieve his suffering.

'Simpson tells me that Aunt Mary is on the way here and will take you home. I shall remain here awhile to gain my strength.'

His voice showed his struggle to talk but Susan detected a forcefulness in his words. He had become more mature now from his experiences. He was clearly too weak for her to remain longer, and needed to rest before Mary came.

Knowing she had not the right of a wife to stay with him and nurse him, she quivered with the agony of having to part from him. But she felt the adventure had matured her, too, and that if she truly loved him, which she did, she must not expect a sick man to think of her welfare any more than he had already.

As his lordship's strength ebbed and his eyes shut in a healing sleep, she let her hand slip from his and walked quietly out of the bedchamber. She'd left him with her heart beating a sad farewell and her eyes stinging with unshed tears, but she knew she was doing what was best for him. When he recovered, if he wanted her, he would find her waiting for him. She would just have to be patient.

* * *

The need to keep occupied when she got back to Bath sent Susan to the library for books to read, and over the winter months she helped with charity work which she found rewarding. She taught Betty to knit which thrilled the maid, and went with her to explore the beautiful city when the weather made it possible.

On a fine day she encouraged Mama to walk along the colonnaded Bath Street and visit the Pump Room. They went to coffee houses and met people they enjoyed chatting to, and when the winter coldness warmed and the flowers of spring appeared with the sunshine, she accompanied her mother and Lady Mary as they strolled by the river.

To her delight, she was accepted without a hint of censure at the few social occasions she attended with

Mama and Lady Mary, and to her surprise her new clothes and gentler manner were appreciated by several gentlemen, who vied for her affection. Some were quite personable, but as her heart was already given, they didn't tempt her. But she was agreeable and pleasant so as not to hurt any young man's feelings.

Little was said about Lord Dearham, although Susan heard he'd been back at Dearham Hall for several weeks.

'We can't expect him to be fit enough to ride yet,' Lady Mary had commented over a game of cards one day. 'Healing takes time. But when I went to visit him last week he was up and about, and suggested we all go and dine with him.'

Lady Lavinia looked over her hand of cards at Susan's blushing face and said, 'Well, it's about time he did.'

But it was not at his grand home that Susan met his lordship again. She was in the Circulating Library and had climbed some steps to see what books lay on the top shelf when she turned and saw him. His long-legged, easy walk and assured air showed that he'd fully recovered from his wounds. His hair was neatly cut in fashionable disarray, in fact Simpson had turned out such a stylish gentleman, he'd attracted the eyes of every lady in the library. Lord Dearham was oblivious to the attention he had created, as he seemed to be looking for someone.

When his eyes finally alighted on Susan, he called in his confident baritone voice, 'Ah, Miss Woodford, I see you are up in the air again!'

His affectionate smile made her lose all sense of time and place, and she almost lost her balance so that the steps rocked dangerously. Having rushed to steady her, he lifted her lightly down to the floor, and seemed in no hurry to release her as they stood looking at each other in delight.

Finding her voice, Susan dispelled the magic moment, as she remembered where she was.

'I'm so pleased to see you well

recovered, my lord.'

'Indeed, and you are looking remarkably well, Miss Woodford.' His eyes twinkled as he offered her his arm saying, 'I suggest we take a stroll outside as the people in here seem more interested in us than in the books!'

She looked up into his kind face, and gave him a dimpled smile, knowing he had chosen to acknowledge her in public. Was it that he wanted to show Society that she was his chosen lady? Susan didn't know for sure, but she hoped he'd come to claim her for his own.

As he walked her home she felt she couldn't ask him where his heart lay, or enquire about his feelings. What about Arabella, or any other lady friends he may have? She only knew that she loved him all the more after their separation, and being close to him again was both a joy, and at the same time frustrating, not knowing where she stood.

In the weeks that followed, he met her frequently, acting as though he were courting her. When they met at private parties or balls, he was most attentive and amusing. Four times she was asked to dinner at Dearham Hall, and they frequently rode in the park together. She looked forward to seeing him almost daily and enjoyed his company very much. They could talk without embarrassment and used their first names, but as the weeks went by Susan began to wonder if he regarded her more like a sister or a cousin, and the idea of taking a lady for his countess had not entered his head.

Yet she felt sure her mama and Lady Mary expected their union. The older ladies irritated her with their constant undercurrent of suggestions, hints and comments that she was soon to be wed. Tom had now adopted the demeanour of a capable and caring member of the landed nobility. Jean-Paul had long since gone back to France, and the fine balloon that was destroyed was not replaced with another. It was almost as if he'd abandoned his youthful hobby.

It seemed as though she'd become his new occupation! But he was tantalising her by not telling her what she most dearly wanted to know. He even took the opportunity to kiss her in private on occasions, which she liked very much, yet felt increasingly dismayed he would not declare his love.

Bath's Spring Garden Ball came on a perfect, summer evening. The ladies had been discussing what they would wear. As well as their gowns, hair dressing was carefully thought about, and perfumes were selected. Younger ladies sighed and prayed their prince would come, while Susan made herself look as ravishing as she could for her lord. Yet she felt tempted to scold him, and tell him that if he didn't want her, he should say so.

Lady Lavinia and Lady Mary had two older gentlemen, family friends, to escort them, and Susan came with them expecting Lord Dearham to appear as he usually did on social occasions. But when he did not, she found herself being pestered by a swarthy, overconfident, and very impertinent foreign gentleman who seemed to think that as she was unescorted she should be willing to partner him. Politely refusing his attentions she could not seem to shake him off and to her dismay she found herself being closely followed.

'Aren't the lights pretty?' Mama exclaimed excitedly, looking at the coloured Chinese lanterns being held by servants, or attached to trees lining the route down to the river where ferrymen were busy rowing people across the water to the gardens where the ball was being held.

The strains of dance music added to the excitement, and the chirpy boatmen were trying their best to keep their betters in order to prevent anyone's fine clothes from being dirtied, or any lively young gentlemen from falling overboard. So a queue of party-goers was having to wait for their turn to be ferried across.

Lord Dearham was head and shoulders above most of the crowd and he soon spotted Susan, looking exquisite in her peach-coloured silk ballgown. Her beloved face, and the way she'd arranged her glossy hair to look so attractive made his stomach turn over. But what he did not like seeing was that leech of a man closely following her.

He realised he'd been courting her for far too long. She was a very desirable woman and watching her he could tell he was not the only man to think so. With a stab of nervousness he realised that if he did not do something about it, he might find she'd choose someone else to marry!

Seeing men eyeing her, especially the gentleman clearly pestering her, made him inwardly seethe. But, outwardly calm, he eased his way through the crowd towards her. The sight of the tall man in his beautifully-tailored clothes and the purposeful look on his handsome face made the crowd step out of his way.

His mind was totally on Susan. Would it not serve him right if she, whom he'd rudely said, only a few months ago, was only fit to marry a hard, army man, refused him now?

His words haunted him as he remembered saying, 'I can't think of a single respectable gentleman who would take you on. It would be more than his life's worth!'

And now he would die for her! His heart was crying out to be near her and to know that she loved him as much as he loved her. With one dismissive look at the gentleman near Susan, his lordship sent the man scurrying off.

Susan heard the much-loved voice at her side and breathed a sigh of pleasure that he'd come at last.

'Tom, how happy I am to see you!'

She dimpled and blushed with delight. How handsome he was in his evening wear, and as she'd become so accustomed to his expressions, she could tell he approved of her carefully put together rig, too.

He seemed a little worried though when he bent to whisper in her ear, 'I've a private boat if you care to come with me.'

Her eyes lifted and met his, and for a moment she was mesmerised.

'Thank you, Tom. But what about Mama and Lady Mary? I seem to have lost them in the crowd.'

'They have their gentlemen in attendance. I've told them I'm claiming you.'

'Oh, have you now!'

She pretended to be shocked, and fluttered her fan.

'Surely they do not approve of me slipping away with you, alone.'

'Don't you trust me?'

'I do, but think of my reputation, my lord!'

He took her arm and walked her away explaining, 'I have been doing so, for far too long. I wanted to show the world that I was courting you correctly. Now I realise I can't wait for you a moment longer, my love, and want you for my wife.'

She stood still and looked up searchingly into his face.

'Am I truly your love, Tom? Or are you just saving me from disgrace?'

'Susan, I love you so much I don't know how I've survived these past few months without having you in my arms. But, do you love me?'

'I will always love you, Tom.'

'I regret I was so rude and teased you when we first met.'

'Did you? I don't remember!'

They laughed, and stopped under the darkness of a spreading oak. She felt his arms capture her, and the sweet touch of his lips on hers. It was supreme bliss.

'Oh, Tom, kiss me for ever,' she said abandoning all restraint.

She felt she was unable to stem the passion he kindled in her, and how extraordinary it was that at one time she'd thought she'd have to marry without love! She knew as they sailed down river in his boat until the strains of music receded, that they had no desire to return for the ball. Cradled together in the darkness they enjoyed their embraces, and laughed as they planned their rosy future.

'I do wonder if you will make another balloon and go flying off into the heavens again,' she asked stroking his hair and kissing his forehead lightly.

'Would you fly with me if I did?'

'Do you know, I think I would!'

THE END

SPECIAL MESSAGE TO READERS

This book is published under the auspices of

THE ULVERSCROFT FOUNDATION

(registered charity No. 264873 UK)

Established in 1972 to provide funds for research, diagnosis and treatment of eye diseases. Examples of contributions made are: —

A Children's Assessment Unit at Moorfield's Hospital, London.

•

Twin operating theatres at the Western Ophthalmic Hospital, London.

•

A Chair of Ophthalmology at the Royal Australian College of Ophthalmologists.

•

The Ulverscroft Children's Eye Unit at the Great Ormond Street Hospital For Sick Children, London.

You can help further the work of the Foundation by making a donation or leaving a legacy. Every contribution, no matter how small, is received with gratitude. Please write for details to:

THE ULVERSCROFT FOUNDATION,
The Green, Bradgate Road, Anstey,
Leicester LE7 7FU, England.
Telephone: (0116) 236 4325

In Australia write to:

THE ULVERSCROFT FOUNDATION,
c/o The Royal Australian College of Ophthalmologists,
27, Commonwealth Street, Sydney,
N.S.W. 2010.